MW01244890

Finally
Gertie

Lacie Minier

Copyright

Trademarks

The author acknowledges the use of the following trademarks:
Starbucks
Target
Red Robin

Cover

Cover designed by Inked Designs

Lacie Minier

My name is Gertie Meyer.

At thirty-eight, I'm perfectly happy being single and living the life of a hermit. Social interaction? Loathe it with a thousand passions. It ranks number one on my list of things to avoid at all costs. The walls around my heart give me the quiet protection I desire until they're shattered one day in a mere blink of an eye. When a man crashes into my life and tries to make me feel again, I realize that I can't fight change, it's inevitable. I don't like it, but what choice do I have when he's helping me accomplish my life's dream? And why is he stirring something inside I'd kept locked in the dark depths of my soul?

My name is Zeke Bradley.

If I was alive, I'd be a forty-year-old man. But no, ever since my life ended eight years ago, my soul has been trapped in limbo. Now I'm the guardian of a woman who is physically alive, but emotionally dead. Helping her become the woman she is meant to be, I might just find the answers to help me move on from my own self-imposed hell. Finally, I've discovered a purpose. It shouldn't be too hard, except Gertie has serious issues with change. Leaving me with quite the task to accomplish, having us both face ourselves.

Lacie Minier

Dedication

For Kyleen

Gertie would not be out of my head and in book form without you. You inspired me, helped me, encouraged me, and supported me through every phase of this book. You put up with my whining, complaining, procrastinating, and pre-caffeinated messages. You have turned into one of my best friends, and I love and appreciate you more than words could express.

Thank you from the bottom of my heart.

Prologue

Gertie

"What are you doing here? I thought you had a date tonight? Did you already ditch the poor soul? Oh Wait, did he die of boredom? Gertie, what am I going to do with you?"

Looking up from where I'm sitting on the couch, Quinn comes into the living room with his bags. He's finally returning from a weeklong trip to Denver for business. Quinn's my best friend and roommate. I consider him my twin. He's the only person who's been able to put up with me for long periods of time. Probably because we've known each other our whole lives. Literally. We were born at the same time in the same hospital room, within minutes of each other, and we haven't been far apart ever since. Granted, I am the only one who can put up with him for longer periods of time too, so that helps.

"He cancelled on me, if you must know. And why's it always *my* fault? Ok, I guess it kind of is this time, but I'm much better off anyway. He apparently didn't like my reply to his text when he suggested we drive over an hour away to go out dancing, in some noisy and 'trendy' club, instead of to dinner and the nice quiet movies."

"Oh, good lord! I can only imagine what you had to say, but please, humor me. What did you respond to him?" Quinn asked while masking a smirk. He knew what was coming. The smartass.

"I told him I'd rather have a root canal with no drugs in the middle of the desert. I thought he'd appreciate that since he's a dentist. Ironically, he didn't. So, an hour later he texted that he had an 'emergency' come in, and he wouldn't be able to make our date. No skin off my ass. I'd much rather stay in anyway."

I wasn't lying. I hate dating. Actually, I hate all forms of social interaction. Loathe it. Avoid it at all costs. My name is Gertie Meyer. I'm a 38-year-old single female who's somewhat a hermit and is totally fine with that. Highly enjoy it.

Quinn drops his bags on the floor and gracefully flops down on the couch beside me. "So, did you eat yet? We could go out."

Looking at him like he's crazy, I wave a hand up and down the front of myself. "Do you not see the jammies? You know the rule. If jammies are on and bra is off, then no going out the rest of the night. So, no. I'm not going out, but I'm all for ordering in. Chinese or pizza?"

Trying desperately to hold in the laugh that is making his whole body quake, he shakes his head at me. "I thought it was worth a try. I mean, it is only 5:30 in the afternoon. You are only thirty-eight. You work from home and don't have a set time you have to be up in the morning. We could leave the apartment and go have a life."

"Why would we want to do that? Did you hit your head on your trip or something? Who am I talking to? What happened to my Quinn who loves to stay in as much as I do?" Joking back at him, as I know he was joking with me. Quinn's just as anti-social and sarcastic as I am. This is why we get along so well. I try to pull off a totally offended look, but it doesn't work and we both just chuckle.

"I know. I don't want to either. I want a long hot bath and food. Wanna do Chinese and movies tonight? I'll go take a bath, then call in the food and we can chill. Sound good?"

"Now you're talking my language. I'll take my usual, please. I'm going to finish this work I was doing when you rudely broke my concentration with your nonsense. Then I'm all yours. First, tell me about your trip. Meet anyone of interest? Get any prospects?"

"For business, yes, I met people and got prospects. You know better than to think I picked someone up. I don't know why you always ask. The answer is always going to be no. I like being by myself. I don't need anyone other than you in my life."

Quinn has it in his head that he isn't good enough for love, or that's what I've gathered over the years. I also think he's a closeted gay, or bisexual, man whose afraid to come out, but again, just my gut instinct. Every time I try to talk to him about it he changes the subject or walks away. It's the only taboo topic between us. Everything else is on the table. He calls himself asexual, but I don't think that is entirely true. I see the spark of interest in his eyes for certain people. He'll figure it out in time. We all do. Just takes some longer than others.

"For the same reason you try to get me to date and conspire with Mom to set me up with lame-ass dentists. Someday, you're going to be totally shocked when someone makes your pulse race and peaks your interest. And personally, I can't wait to be around for it. I can't wait to see your reaction. You, my friend, aren't an island, and you'll find your soulmate. I have faith in it."

"Hey, Mom and I have your best interests at heart. How about you? When you going to go looking for your 'soulmate'?"

"Nope. Not going to happen. I'm too lazy. If there's a missing piece of a puzzle in my life, the universe better drop him in my lap. I don't do searching. Bring him to me."

Quinn quaked with laughter. "You're too much, you lazy ass. Well, same for me. I don't have time to go looking. Let the universe drop them in my lap, too. I have too many jobs and designs to do to go searching for something that I know isn't out there for me." Patting my leg, Quinn stands and heads to his room.

My heart aches for him. He needs someone to love him. I do and can, but only so much. He deserves the love and affection his Mom never gave him. Plus, he is my BFF. My twin. I want to see him happy. Knowing he isn't, and never has been, hurts me. I haven't experienced that type of happiness either. This is why we're so close.

This is the bad thing about being an empath. I can't distance myself from the feelings of my loved ones. If they're sad, even the smallest amount, I feel it. I just want to help them and most of the time, I can't. People have to help themselves. That's a big lesson that took a long time to grasp. That's why I blocked off my heart and walled it up. The less I feel of myself, the less I feel of others. I learned that at an early age. Plus, then I didn't get made fun of by other kids when I made comments about things I shouldn't know, but did, because of

11

my "gift". It's not easy to make friends when you're "different" as a kid. Kind of sucks to be honest. Thankfully, Quinn never cared and wasn't scared of me.

Turning back to my laptop, I get back to work so I can enjoy time with Quinn tonight. We both need a night to relax, eat, and watch movies. Both of us work so hard at our freelance businesses that we forget to take time off to relax. Tonight, I'll make sure we do just that.

Chapter 1

Gertie

Three months later.

Standing by the door, I'm waiting for Quinn as he finally strolls out of his bedroom in black jeans and a cobalt blue button-down shirt that make his eyes pop.

"Gertie, I can't believe I actually talked you into going out, and I can't believe I actually want to. But we need to celebrate. I'm in shock that I won the big decorating job at the bed and breakfast they're building downtown. This is so exciting. I just have to get out of here and do something with all this energy!"

Giving Quinn a big hug, I can't help but smile. This is the happiest I've ever seen him. "I can't believe you call it downtown like Raineyville is huge or something. I am so proud of you! Let's go. Dinner's on me. Only thing, you have to drive. I don't like driving at night."

"That's fine with me. Let's go."

After a dinner at the best restaurant in our little town, we drive about thirty minutes away to the closest big city around, and end up at a little café that has live acoustic music. We've been sitting towards the back, away from the crowd, for the last hour nursing our one glass of wine each. Neither of us are interested in drinking to get drunk, but it's usually because we're wussies and don't like feeling hungover the next day. I much prefer watching everyone else get drunk and act stupid. Back in college, I learned I liked watching the antics of the others instead of being one of the drunk, stupid people that feels like ass the next day.

"This guy is really good. I don't know if these are original songs or covers, but I really like him." Quinn whispers in my ear. I nod my head in agreement.

This guy has a smoky-deep, soulful voice that I would expect on a man much bigger than his size. "I think this is an old Johnny Cash song; I love it."

We listen quietly to the rest of the set and enjoy the night. Heading home about 1:30 in the morning, I fall asleep for most of the drive, but wake up as we get closer to home. "Hey sleepy head. How was your power nap?"

"Very funny. I would still be out if you didn't hit that pothole. When are they going to fix that?"

"No clue. Holy shit. Hold on!"

Looking over to where Quinn is staring, I see a car coming straight at us. "Shit!"

Chapter 2

Gertie

I wake up, or I think I do, in a place that I have a vague sense of remembering… but I have no clue why. Feeling foggy and light, almost airy, I look down at my hands noticing they're transparent. Ok. Well, that's weird, even for me.

Looking around, everything is transparent. There are bright colored flowers, lilies and daisies mostly, everywhere. Standing in the middle of an open grassy area next to a pond and waterfall, there's a bench about six feet away with a man sitting on it watching me. He doesn't feel threatening, kind of familiar actually, but I hate people staring at me. It's a little creepy since he's a transparent figure. A ghost? Geez, what the hell's going on?

"Uh, what? Why are you staring at me? And, um, who are you?"

The man smiles and I swear I hear angels singing somewhere. How frigging cliché is that? But seriously, in my life this has never happened. Is it normal? I hate to admit that I have no clue. None. Zero. Zip.

He has the most beautiful green eyes, they are large, vibrant and framed with illegally long eye lashes, and the dimple in his right cheek makes my muscles melt. Damn. At this point, I don't care who he is or where I am. This is already better than my shitty-ass life.

"I could have sworn your first question was going to be 'where am I' but hey, we can play this your way. My name is Zeke. I don't know exactly where we are, but let's just say it isn't earth. I'm not sure why I'm here to answer your questions, but you're here because you were in an auto accident, and your body is in a hospital bed in a comatose state. This is a safe place for your soul to hang out while your physical body deals with everything it was put through and to heal. You and I've been paired together to figure out if it's your time to come back to the soul realm, or if you have more time and work to do in the 'human

15

earthly realm'. I have no clue if these are the right words for these things; I'm going by the seat of my pants here. And to answer your other question, I'm staring at you because you seem so familiar to me, and I can't figure out why. Your eyes are beautiful, by the way. Even in the transparent state they are so blue."

Well damn. Mr. Green Eyes thinks my eyes are beautiful. Screw going back. I'm staying here with him. Taking a minute to get past the first compliment I've ever received from a man, I begin to process what he said.

"Ok. Not sure what to address first... so, um, thank you for the compliment?" Taking a deep breath and another minute to ponder everything he just said, I look out over the flowers, pond and waterfall. I was in a car accident? Oh shit! I was with Quinn. "Was anyone else hurt? How's Quinn?" I ask in a panic, as I rub the pain I got in my chest from the possibility he was hurt.

"Quinn's going to be fine. He broke his left arm, but otherwise, he was treated and released. You're the one who got hit directly. Other than the brain swelling which caused the coma, you have a couple broken bones, and a broken rib that punctured a lung. They're ensuring you stay in the coma, medically, till your lungs are more healed and the swelling in your brain goes down, so you don't move around and cause more damage. The drunk driver in the other car died on impact."

Letting out a huge sigh that Quinn's ok, I can't decide what I want to ask next. Too many questions are in my head, so I do what I always do without thinking, go with the most unimportant ones first. "How do you know all this if you're not human, or are you? What are you?"

Shaking his head, which moves his dark curls all around his head, Zeke sighs. It's hypnotic to watch those lovely curls just sway back and forth. Well, that is something new that I've never noticed about a guy before. Huh. What the hell is wrong with me? Oh, right. Brain injury.

"I have no clue, Gertie. It just comes to me. As soon as you ask a question, I'm granted the answer to tell you. I hear it in my head. I'm new to this so bear with me. Although, I feel like I've done this before, but can't remember when or how. It's so screwed up. I feel more confused than anything else right now. I've absolutely no clue how to explain it."

Chuckling at the confusion written all over his face, a sense of relief washes over me knowing that I'm not the only one who is lost in what's happening. "So, it's like the blind leading the blind here, huh?"

He smiles. Holy shit. He *really* needs to stop doing that. It's making me melt and feel all funny inside, which is very much *not* me. I'm not sure I like this feeling. It's new and foreign, and I don't like new and foreign. I always thought it would be a nauseous feeling, if it actually happened, but instead I feel warm and tingly in a good way from that smile. Huh, interesting and unsettling. Can I still blame the brain injury for this one?

"Unfortunately, yes. We get to work things out together; I hope you like sarcasm because I tend to overdue...or at least I did when I was in human form. Who knows what happens up here? You're the first person, soul, whatever, that I've run into since I got here."

Zeke looks around at everything with a look on his face I couldn't place. Kind of a frown of sorts. Frustration? Confusion? Longing? A mix of all? I can't tell. I can't tap into his energy like I can with others. That's new, refreshing in a way, but new.

"How long have you been wherever here is?"

Sighing again, Zeke looks down at the ground and rubs his face in his palms. Noticing that he has no shoes on, I can't help but admire his long, slim feet. His nails are perfectly trimmed and shiny and his toes are long and slender. I can't believe I'm going to say this, but wow, this man has beautiful feet. OMG, seriously, what's happening to me?

"Gertie, I have no clue. It feels like forever, yet it also feels like an hour. I can't explain it. It's like time doesn't exist here. I've been wandering around this area since I arrived with no purpose or reason. I feel like a lost soul. Every time I ask out loud what I'm doing here, I hear in my head 'It will all be revealed at the right time. Have faith.' from this mysterious deep voice. And I want to get frustrated, but apparently you aren't allowed to do that here because I feel nothing. Numb. That's all I've been since I got here. Not peaceful or happy or anything. Just Numb. In my head I know I'm frustrated, but I don't feel it. Really, I can't explain it. I wish I could."

"I think I can understand. I've felt nothing but numb all my life. Most people don't get it. They think I'm robotic. I openly admit to making it that way myself though. It's safer for me." Looking around again, I fully take in the beauty of this place. I think I could enjoy just hanging out here with nothing to do. Stress free and people free. Just the waterfall, the flowers and this beautiful man as a companion. Hell yeah, I could totally love that. His energy feels familiar to me, and it's warm and comforting, but I don't like that I can't feel what he's thinking. Huh, I hate that in my normal life, and yet, I want it with him?

We sit in silence for a while. I can't help but ask, because I instantly feel he would know what I feel, "Have you ever felt alone, even when you're in a room full of people and family? Like no one understands you at all. Or like you're missing something in your life, and you've no clue what it is or how to find it?" These are always my big hang-ups in life. The worst of the feelings that I try to suppress on a daily basis.

Smiling sadly, he nods at me and looks back down at the ground. "Yep. That was my whole last life. Every single minute of it. That's why I took my own life and ended up here."

Holy crap. Did I really just hear that? "You killed yourself? How? Why?"

Zeke looked at me sadly, then out to the waterfall. "I'm not sure if I should actually tell you, but what the heck. Wait? Really, I can't swear? Darn it! AUGH!" Looking around like he's looking for someone to holler at for this revelation, he holds his hands out in front of himself.

I feel the bubble of laughter tickle my stomach and work its way out of me. "OK, I can't stay here if I can't swear. That's a deal breaker." Because seriously, that is a main way I express myself. They're sentence enhancers.

Laughing at me again, Zeke smiles. "Right? Well heck. Ok, fine. Anyway, yeah I did. I got so fed up with the life my father was pushing me into and the feeling like something was missing that I could never find. I never felt like I fit in anywhere or with anyone. I was so lonely, even though everyone seemed to 'love me'. I was really good at hiding my feelings and thoughts. No one knew how I felt. No one ever asked or seemed to notice. I kept it all inside and one day it became too much. My roommate was diabetic. I took one of his syringes and got his insulin out of the frig and injected myself. Apparently, they never figured out how I died or just didn't care enough to figure it out. But I just couldn't take it anymore."

"I totally get that. I've never thought about suicide before, for myself, but I understand why someone would do it. I often wonder if I'll ever find any kind of happiness that fills the eternally empty spot within me, if I'll ever feel complete. I've no motivation in life other than my work, which I throw myself into. And even that doesn't give me real satisfaction anymore. It is just a time passer. I don't think I've ever found anything that gives me satisfaction in anyway, other than Freddy. He's my therapy dog. Someday I would love to write a book and have it published, then I can say I did something I wanted to do instead of just helping others with their books. I want to make a difference, but don't know how to do it and I don't have the motivation to figure it out. I always think 'Who would want to read what I've got to say, and who would really care'?"

He nods and I know he understands exactly what I mean, and how I feel. It's in his eyes, the pain, the camaraderie in feeling this way, the understanding. We once again settle into quietness as we stare out at the waterfall.

A light bell rings once. Zeke looks up and then at me. "It's almost time for you to go back; we have to figure out what we have to do. *They*, whoever *they* are, decided for you that you're not ready to come here yet. I'm assuming I'm paired with you because you feel the same way I did. Maybe I'm to help you have the life we both wanted?"

Thinking on what he said, do I really want to go back? Being here with him feels more right and comfortable than I have ever experienced. I realize that here with him, I think I could be happy. I'm content right now. I feel light and stress-free. I really don't want to leave.

Before I even get to say anything, Zeke shakes his head, "I'm sorry, Gertie, but I'm being told you have to go, at least this time. Don't worry, I get to be with you, to help you through your life this time. I'll be there when you need me. Just start talking to me in your head or out loud, and I'll answer. You may or may not see me, but you'll hear me or just 'know' my answer."

Sighing in regret over having to leave, I do what I do best and resort to humor and sarcasm. "If I have to. I'm going to feel funny talking to nothing though. Are you going to watch me shower if I accidentally think something to you while I'm in there?"

Biting back a chuckle, Zeke shakes his head at me, yet again. "No to the shower. That's just wrong Gertie. But, yeah, sorry to you having to go back. Nothing I can do about that or the talking to yourself. Suck it up, buttercup. Oh! Hey, I got it!"

Turning to me with an excited glimmer in his eyes, "Go back and write our story. We both have felt the same way in life. Tell others how we feel and that they are not alone. I can't help but think there are many others out there that feel the same way. Maybe we can make a difference in someone's life so they don't take their life like I did. What do you think? Should we try to save someone else?"

Looking at him, I see the pleading in his eyes. Deep down, I know that this will not only save him, but help me achieve a goal of my own. I can feel it in my gut that this idea is the right one for us. The tingling that starts with his smile now moves slowly through my body. Excitement? Is that what it feels like? "Ok. But I don't know your full story. How can I write it?"

Zeke smiles again, and I feel myself melt just a little more. My body should be a pile of pudding on the ground by now. A buzzing is vibrating through my body that wasn't there before, or ever. Seriously, is this what emotions feel like?

"You will Gertie. I'll make sure that you know my story. Keep a notebook by your bed. I'll visit you in dreams and we can talk. I want you to fulfill your dream and I need to help you. For you and for me. Maybe it can help me to move on. We need each other, Gertie. Does this make any kind of sense?" Shrugging in what appears to be frustration that he can't explain it better, Zeke looks back out to the waterfall.

I smile at him. I don't understand any of this either, but it feels right. It all makes me feel content and less twitchy than normal. "Yeah, I think it does."

Feeling a stabbing pain in my chest, I grab ahold of the bench. "What the hell?"

Zeke is disappearing, I vaguely hear him say "Oh sure, you can swear! So not fair. Gertie, you're going back. It isn't going to be an easy rehab, but remember, I'm always here...."

Hearing nothing else, I start to feel pain everywhere in my body. Damnit, why couldn't I stay at that beautiful place with that beautiful man? Seriously, this is just my luck.

Opening my eyes, I see a worried Quinn staring at the wall biting his nails. As much as I want to soothe him, I can't seem to move. Pain is shooting everywhere, my arms feel like dead weights and I can't seem to lift them. I shift my head to the side, and the movement is enough to get his attention.

"Holy shit! Finally, Gertie. You scared the hell out of me! Let me get a nurse. It's about damned time you wake your lazy ass up."

I can't help but giggle internally. That's my Quinn, all worried and shit about little old me. Nodding my head briefly, I feel dizzy. Ok, note to self, don't do that again for a while. I'm afraid to try to talk. Not sure why, but it doesn't seem like it's going to work and it might hurt. Still feeling like I'm in a fog, I'm awake enough to know that they must have had a tube down my throat for a decent amount of time, which means my throat is going to hurt. Ironically, it is the one thing I feel no pain in currently. Why change that?

Closing my eyes again, I wait. I mean seriously, what else do I have to do? Knowing there's going to be a bunch of poking and prodding now that I'm awake, I'm not sure I'm up for it. I should have just played dead a while longer. Ok, probably not the best way to think of it, but hell, I hurt. A lot. I want to go back to Zeke in the beautiful meadow where I didn't feel pain, but where I was starting to feel foreign things. So now that I am back here, where is the comfortably numb feeling that I usually have? I want that back. I am a wuss. I don't like pain. At all.

Just as I thought, I hear people come in and start gathering things. One of them touches my arm and I open my eyes. A nice, sweet looking redhead is smiling down at me and I feel better, like I'll be in good hands. I like her energy, it soothes me a little bit. "Honey, I know these things are going to hurt, but we have to look you over and ask you some questions to evaluate you for possible brain damage and memory loss. You're going to hate me and Dr. Roots in about 5 minutes, but I promise to be nice to you for the rest of the night and treat you well." She winks at me and I decide that I can put up with it for her. I like her.

I smile back at her. I nod, and again feel dizzy. "What's your name?" I squeak out. Not as much pain as I thought, but I sound like a bullfrog.

"Oh honey, try not to talk unless we ask you questions. Your throat is still healing from the tube that was down it. My name is Tracy. I'm with you till 8:00 am, then I'll be back at 8:00 pm for the overnight with you again."

"Ok. Dizzy when I nod. Feel better talking."

"Ok, honey. I'll give the Dr. that information. But still, try to hold your voice for the important questions later, ok?" I slowly lift my right arm about an inch and give her a thumbs up. Surprisingly, that didn't hurt as much as I feared. It feels heavy, but not too bad right now.

After about a half an hour of them drawing more blood, poking me at certain spots, and multiple questions, they have deemed me ok with memory and no 'real' brain damage. That relaxes me, and they finally let me rest again. Quinn has been unusually quiet the whole time. He's sitting on the bed next to me, holding my hand and staring at the TV.

"How long have I been out?"

Quinn still looks worried even though he heard the doctor say I would be ok. "About 6 weeks. I was starting to wonder if you were ever coming back."

"Of course, Quinn. I wouldn't leave you, yet. How are you? Were you Ok?"

"I have a broken left arm, but I'm fine and it's almost healed. Let's just worry about you."

Nodding, I look around the room again. "Where's Mom and Dad?" I squeak out.

"Oh, I sent them home around 9 to shower and sleep. They'll be back in the morning."

"What time is it?" I look around, but my room doesn't have a window or a clock.

"Sweetie, it's like two o'clock in the morning. You always were a night owl."

"Haha. Why are you still here then? You should be home sleeping."

He smiles sadly at me, and it about breaks my heart. "I couldn't leave you. The apartment is too quiet, and my head is too loud. I had to be here until you woke up. I was so worried you wouldn't. God Gertie, I really thought you were gone. I'll never admit this again, but I was so scared. Uh, oh and I sent Freddie and Petunia to your sisters till you come home. Freddie isn't happy without you."

My heart breaks for Quinn. My family and I are all he has in this world other than Petunia. I know he was driving the car, and I also remember there was nothing he could have done to prevent what happened. The other driver went through a red light that had been red already for almost a full minute. Even though Quinn saw him coming, there was nowhere for him to swerve to avoid being hit. It was only about three seconds, if that, from the moment we saw him coming and impact, but it felt like an hour. Knowing Quinn well enough, I understand that he feels guilty about it anyway. I also know him well enough to know there is nothing I can say to make him feel better until I get out and he sees me moving around and okay again.

"Quinn, I'm here. I'm back and I love you. I wouldn't want anyone else to sit with me till I get out of here. Stay, Ok?"

Sighing with relief, he gives me a true smile. Relaxing, he leans forward and kisses my forehead. "Wouldn't think of leaving you sweetie. I haven't since that horrible day. Now get some rest."

Nodding slightly, I shut my eyes. Oh, beautiful sleep.

Lacie Minier

Chapter 3

Gertie

Over the last 2 weeks, I've been moved to a regular room and put through physical therapy for my broken bones. They taught me how to walk and cope with my injuries until they heal. Poor Quinn's going to have his hands full with me when they release me tomorrow. Good thing his arm is healed.

I've had two dreams with Zeke where we just sit and talk. Mostly, they're about nothing important. It feels like he's just keeping me company until I heal. He hasn't yet told me about his life, but we are getting to know each other better through our conversations. He asked me last night about the basic stuff like food, drinks, bands, and all my other favorites. Sometimes I wake up feeling more tired and like I haven't rested at all. We always meet at the same location, what I like to think of as 'our spot', on the bench beside the waterfall and bright wildflowers.

I've started to associate a certain smell with Zeke. I can't quite place it, but it's very familiar. I like the smell and like knowing when he's around, even when I'm awake. It soothes me and helps me relax. Here's an example: At the hospital, they took me for another scan in the machine that had given me a panic attack the first time. They had to give me a really fun drug to calm me down. The drug made me feel all light and airy. Everything looked vivid and like it was floating. I will fully admit to liking that drug and that feeling, but it wasn't as calming as the second time they took me for the scan. I only had to smell Zeke's presence to know he was there, and I instantly relaxed and was okay.

Strange? Hell yes. Disconcerting? Not in the least. I feel more comfortable and relaxed with him around, even if he isn't visible. I am really starting to wonder if the doctor made a mistake about me not having lasting brain damage. How can this be normal?

I still can't quite put my finger on why the presence of a man I have never met until now, and honestly, still don't know if he is real or just a figment of my brain injury, puts me at ease so quickly. But hey, it works. Placebo effect? Possibly. But it works, and I'm running with it. Maybe I'm fully crazy and not just half like I always thought, but if it works to help me, then so be it. I need some damn calm in my life, and especially, in my head.

It's odd to me how much Zeke's thoughts and feelings mirror mine. It's almost like the core of our emotions are exactly the same. How is that possible since we are different in family backgrounds and personality? He was extroverted and outgoing in life, or so it seems thus far. I'm a damned socially awkward hermit who talks only to Quinn, my family, and my clients; I basically only speak to people when I have to. Zeke had tons of friends surrounding him, and I have Quinn and Freddy.

Yet, more importantly, we both feel alone and only half of a whole. We both feel like something is missing and we don't even know what the missing piece is to describe it. How do you go about finding something when you don't know what it is? Where do you even start?

While staring out the window contemplating all of this, Quinn returns with the Starbucks I insisted he go get me. I'm going through mocha withdrawals something nasty, and he really needed fresh air after all the time he's spent in the hospital with me. Coming up to the bed, he hands me my piece of heaven and kisses my forehead. His signature move. "Here you go sweetie. Black and white mocha, 2 pumps each, kids temp and no whip. Did I get it right?"

Oh man, it smells orgasmic! "Quinn, I love you so hard right now. You got it completely correct, like always, and honestly you don't understand how much I need this to feel human again." I take a huge sip and cherish the feeling of the warm liquid sliding over my tongue and down my throat. I love this moment. The first sip of my favorite coffee drink. It appears like life is starting to return to normal. Well normal for me. There's seriously nothing as good in life as that first sip of a good coffee, especially when you haven't had one in way too long. I really can't express that enough. "Oh man, this is seriously heaven."

Quinn just smiles at me and mumbles "coffee whore" before taking a sip of his own. Chuckling, I gladly accept that nickname. My middle name should be coffee or mocha. Really. I would wear that bitch proudly. "So, when are they springing me tomorrow? Are you sure you don't mind taking care of me? I can have Mom come over or get the visiting nurses they mentioned."

Sitting up in his chair, Quinn shakes his head at me. "Nope. All me. I'm more than willing to help my Gertie get healthy. Me and the animals are all ready for you. I got groceries delivered from Amazon, thank you wifi, and your Mom even cleaned up your room so you won't trip over anything. We're ready to bring you home, coffee whore."

"Good. I can't wait to get home. I miss my Freddie something awful. I can't believe they wouldn't let him in here. He's a damned therapy dog for fucks sake. I mean, what the hell? That's his job!"

Quinn rolls his eyes. He knows how grouchy I get without my Freddie, and I know that he was just as mad when Freddie was denied access. I heard him screaming up a storm at the nurses outside my door during that conversation. "I should've just snuck him in in a bag."

Lacie Minier

Chapter 4

Gertie

"So Zeke, I can't write your story if I don't know it. Tell me a little about yourself." I say as I sit back on the bench, cross my right leg over my left one and tap my pen against my lips. We are chit chatting in our spot on the bench. I feel so light and carefree when I am here. There is something about this place that calms something inside me.

Turning his head to look at me, Zeke starts laughing. "You sound like a darn shrink. How am I supposed to open up to you when you act like that? Don't you want to make me feel all comfortable, and warm and fuzzy instead? And this is a dream, how do you have a pen?"

Looking down at it, I twirl the pen in question and look back at him "I don't have a clue. How are we sitting on this bench? Where did this bench come from? Will it always be here? Where is here? If we start asking too many questions we're going to get nowhere but frustrated and waste time. Talk sucker. Stop stalling. What do I need to know about you?"

Looking me dead in the eye, he sighs. There go the butterflies again. The damned things just started a dance-off party in my stomach. Feeling like I'm slowly sliding off the bench, I get that melty feeling in my muscles. What the hell?

"Yeah I guess you're right. I probably can't move on till I work through this, and I can't do that till I talk to you. But, I've kind of grown fond of you. I don't want you to see, or in this case hear, the bad in me. Is that cheesy or what?"

Laughing at him, I look over to see if he looks serious. "Zeke you're full of shit. We haven't spent that much time together except in the hospital, how could you have 'grown fond of me'? I call bullshit on that excuse. Talk buddy. Don't make me pull out my super-ninja psychology skills on you."

Seriously? Am I really this cheesy? Or does he bring it out in me? Super-Ninja Psychology skills? What is wrong with me?

Laughing at me again, Zeke shakes his head. I notice he does that a lot. I get the feeling he doesn't know what to do with me and the way I talk to him. I kind of like that idea, keep him on his toes. Although in all honesty, I don't know what to do with me either.

"Ok. Fine. But I've been watching over you, and I've gotten to know you through those observations. Don't question it. I'm being serious. You're *interesting* to say the least. You make me laugh and that's something I never did much of in my lifetime. Ok, where do I start?"

Sitting quietly for a moment, Zeke has a look on his face that I can only believe means he's deep in thought. His eyes take on a vacant look, kind of hopeless. Rubbing his hands over his face, he takes a deep breath. As he turns to look at me, he lets out a long sigh.

"I have no clue where to start, so I'm just going to start with telling you family basics I haven't already told you, and we'll see where it goes. I was the oldest of three kids. The only boy. I was good at sports, so Dad had me involved in everything, whether I wanted to play or not. I was a very shy kid but was pushed into playing every sport there was in our area. I grew up in a rural town in the Midwest. Typical farmland country. My Dad's a supervising manager/executive type at the local manufacturing company that packaged and shipped corn. Typical, right? My Mom's a school teacher. God, I feel like such a stereotype, but it's true. My sisters were little princesses. They weren't allowed to get dirty, and I wasn't allowed to stay clean."

He looks out over the waterfall. I notice a hint of shame, maybe, cross his face. Without being able to tap into his energy, I feel at a loss for picking up his emotions.

"Gertie, I know I shouldn't feel this way, and it makes me feel guilty, but I hated it. Just because I was good at the sports he had me involved in, didn't mean I wanted to be a part of them. I just wanted to stay at home to read and paint. I loved to paint, but Dad wouldn't buy me the stuff to do it. He thought that was for females and 'soft men'. Not hard sports guys like myself. I didn't need to be creative because I was a 'strapping young man'. I hated that so much. I would sneak supplies that my sisters would buy for me into my room. I learned to put on a façade of being friendly and having friends. I was a total fraud. It was all an act. Honestly, no one really knew me at all. I barely talked to anyone, but everyone seemed to consider me their friend. Because of the teams I played on, I was always part of the popular group."

Feeling a ping of hurt in my heart, I didn't realize how much Zeke had carried with him. This type of life sounds like it sucked. I understand where the pressure started in his life, and it grew as time went on. Moving closer to him on the bench, I give him time to reflect and talk at his own speed. I mean, I am dreaming, right? Not like I have anywhere else to go right now.

Is this real? Who knows. Do I care? Nope. I don't think I do. I'm happy here so why overthink it?

"I kept my grades up in hopes I wouldn't have to take a scholarship to pay for college, but my Dad didn't give me a choice. I ended up going to college in Michigan for football and baseball. I picked there to get far away from the family, to try to have more freedom. Didn't work though. I wanted to major in art and journalism but wasn't allowed. Can you believe that crap? I wasn't allowed to do what I wanted. I was told what I would do. And I did it. I rolled over and let him put me in the Athletic Training program so I could still have a career in something sports related, if I didn't get picked up by the pros. Nice huh? Yeah, just what I wanted to do. Be around annoying jocks, who I hated by the way, and play something I detested all my life till I was hurt in a game and had to get a real job. No amount of money is worth being that unhappy and doing something you hate. I know that now. The guys I was around in locker rooms, my teammates, were totally two faced, closed minded idiots. At least the ones I ran into were."

Nodding in understanding, I feel like my heart is breaking while listening to what he went through. I can only imagine how isolating and self-defeating that would be to let someone else run your life, plan your future, and you give in and let it happen.

"Yeah Zeke, the ones I ran into in school were, too. I played, well tried to play tennis in high school and played intermural volleyball in college. I was good at volleyball. It was a two-person team; my roommate and I played together. We kicked ass, but there was a lot of typical jocks there and I couldn't stand them. My roommate was a lesbian so they thought it was free reign to pick on her. It pissed me off. She was used to it and never cared, but I did. It was obnoxious. And I let them know they were rude and spiked the ball in their faces. That shut them up quickly." I smile proudly at that memory. I had a mean spike.

"Yep, put up with that crap all my life. They were nasty and downright mean when they wanted to be. So close minded, and all because that's the way their parents taught them to be. That's why I learned to stay quiet and act normal. Just try to be their friend. The more of a wallflower I was, the better I felt in the chaos that was my life. I never felt good or great, but I could manage that way."

Taking a long, deep breath, Zeke pressed on. "The girls thought I was the 'strong and silent type' or 'dark and mysterious' and fawned all over me. I hated that too, because I knew they didn't care about the real me. They didn't care who I was deep down. All they cared about was that I was popular and a good ball player. I was the 'perfect guy' who everyone wanted for that reason only. I never dated in high school or college for that reason. No one ever knew the real me. No one tried to get to know the real me. Heck, I'm not even sure I ever knew the real me. I still question who I am, and I technically 'am' no longer."

"That's not true. You're a soul so you exist, just not the same way you did before. You mean you still don't know the real you, your soul or essence."

Zeke looked at me like I just hit him over the head with a brick. "Huh, I never thought about that. I assumed that I didn't need to figure out who I was since I wasn't in human form anymore."

"Ok, I don't know what this place is or anything about the afterlife, although I feel like I have been here multiple times before..." Looking around again, I hope some memory will come up but nothing does. I smell the flowers and hear the water. But no memories. "But I digress...so isn't the main reason we go into human form to learn and grow as a soul? If that's true, what did you learn in this last life? Or what do you think you were supposed to learn? What were you meant to accomplish?"

As I ask him this question, I can't help but wonder where it came from. This isn't something I recall thinking about before. I have edited books on this topic, but never sat down and pondered it myself. I need to ask myself these questions. What am I doing here this time around? What is my purpose? Do I even believe I have one? Damn it. I really don't need more going on in my head. Deep thoughts with Gertie Meyer...

"Gertie, are you sure that you're the one who's still in human form? I think you're smarter than I am, and I'm the soul who's been hanging around up here for who knows how long. Ok, you know that is a darn good question. Dang it. I still hate that I can't swear. This fudging stinks."

I can't help laughing at the exasperated look on Zeke's lovely face. The fact that I laugh so full and heartedly with Zeke is almost scary. I don't even laugh this hard with Quinn. I want to blame the light and content feeling I have when I'm up here on Zeke too, but I've no clue if that's truly the reason. This 'feeling' stuff is so foreign. I mean what? Am I going to get emotions next? Will I get a handle on these things? Good gravy, why are these things happening to me? Numbness, why do you forsake me?

"So you swore a lot in life, Zeke? Drop the good ole f-bombs?"

Zeke gives me a killer smile that about takes my breath away. Wow. My heart starts racing like cars in the Indy 500, and the butterflies have taken the dance party to a whole new level. I can't believe that I've never felt these things before, and here I am talking to a dead guy and getting all "femalely". Yeah. This sucks as much as it's exciting. Melty feelings, pulse racing, tummy turning. Just. My. Luck. I totally understand why girls chased him, even though he doesn't. Yep. Totally get it. I would strap on running shoes and take up track for that smile.

Damn, maybe I'm more normal then I thought? Nope. That's highly doubtful. I'm still going with undiagnosed long-term brain injury. The brain controls hormones and chemicals in your body, right?

"Oh yeah. I did it to annoy my parents in the beginning, but it became a habit I couldn't stop. It was my one rebellion against my parents. Plus, it always just felt good to let one out."

I laugh, "Yeah, it's a nice stress reliever. A well emphasized swear word can make you feel better. At least for me it does. Going outside and screaming one at the top of my lungs, better, and cheaper than any therapy."

He smiles again. Holy shit, why is he taunting me? Do men do this on purpose? Can he tell what it does to me? And how does he get his teeth that white? Do they groom up here or are they just blessed with beautiful everything? I have to know.

"So, did you look like this in human form? Such white teeth? Perfectly styled hair? Because with that dimple I can totally see why the girls would chase after you, and it wasn't just because you were popular or played sports."

He breaks out into a big belly laugh that warms my heart and sets the butterflies flying and dancing again. Damnit. He has to know what it does to me, right? Why do I even care? I hate how foreign this all is and that I don't know if this is normal. How did I get this far in life without knowing these feelings, and not knowing whether he can tell how it affects me?

"Heck, I don't know what you're looking at. I have no clue how you see me. No mirrors up here, you know? Apparently, people view each of us up here differently. Per how we sense them from their energy or their feel or something. As you get to know a soul, the presence can change or something like that. I don't understand it all. I was about six feet tall and around two-hundred pounds. I was leaner muscled thanks to Dad and the training he put me through all the fudging time, but I wasn't overly muscular. Except I had huge thighs. I never could find jeans that fit right. That used to drive me bat crap crazy."

Pausing, Zeke holds his hands around his legs to show how big they used to be, I'm assuming.

"I had crap brown hair. Like any average hair color and style, I guess. Brown eyes and no dimples. I was completely average in looks. I blended in like any normal looking Midwestern kid. I did have a baby face though, with freckles. I was hoping to outgrow those but never seemed to. How do you see me? Other than the dimple, of course."

Taking the opportunity to thoroughly look him over, I hate to admit that I enjoy the view a lot more than I have any other male I've seen. Zeke makes me all tingly and warm. Is that supposed to happen? Maybe it's because of how fast my blood is pumping. Yeah, that makes sense.

"You're about the same height and build probably, but you have the brightest green eyes I've ever seen and really dark brown curly hair, almost black. It's a little on the longer side so it moves when you move your head. You have higher cheekbones that look cut from granite, and a dimple in your right cheek. You also have an ass chin, but damned if you don't pull it off better than anyone else I've ever seen."

He sputters out a laugh that makes me shiver with goosebumps. Really? This is getting ridiculous. Now I am apparently cold? Why else get goosebumps?

"A what? What's a butt chin?"

"You know, a dimple like thingy in your chin." I try to give myself one by pinching my chin skin together, and he starts laughing even harder. Seriously, he needs to stop doing that! It is making me feel all funny. Squirming around in my seat, I feel a little uncomfortable. All these foreign sensations are starting to unsettle me.

"I've never heard it called that before! I don't think I knew it had any type of name. But no, this is not how I looked in life. Huh, I wonder what this description says about how you see my soul? Anyway, my full name was Zeke Bradley. Straight Zeke, not short for anything. Research it on the internet and you'll probably find a photo somewhere. My roommate, Roman, was big on pictures and being on all those teams, there has to be a picture somewhere in cyberspace. I was in college in the late 90's, early 2000's and died in 2011. What year is it anyway?"

"2018. How old were you when you died?"

"Wow, I would have turned forty this year. Huh. Oh, sorry, I was thirty-two and a half or so, I think. I never really paid attention after twenty-one. It meant nothing to me really. Holy crap. How is it I suddenly feel old even though I'm not? Or am I? Do I age up here like I would have down there? Man, this is so weird. How old are you anyway?"

"I'm thirty-eight. Not much younger than you, I guess? I hope this doesn't bother you, but did they ever figure out that you took your own life? You hinted before that you wanted to keep it a mystery."

Looking away from me and out to the waterfall, his face morphs into the expression from before. Shame, maybe? Guilt? I hate that I can't sense what he's feeling. I also don't like that I don't like it. There's a lot I'm not liking in this dream.

"My sisters believe I did, but my parents won't even talk about it. The medical examiner marked it as a natural death and never did an autopsy. So no, no one ever knew for sure. I get the feeling my Dad paid to have it that way, no one looking into it further. He wouldn't want people to know that his perfect son wasn't perfect and did something to disgrace the family. God forbid!"

Shaking his head, he paused. This time, disgust is written all over his face.

"I was hoping they wouldn't figure it out anyway. I had my life insurance set to divide between my sisters, Abbey and Mandy. I wanted them to get the money. They were pushed into lives and marriages they didn't seem to want either. Consider it my consolation prize to them for having to deal with our parents. I thought the money may help them move on if they wanted to do so. None of us got to do what we wanted when we were younger. I just hope they have better outcomes. We were never too close, but they're still family. They're still my little sisters, and I felt the need to try to take care of them as much as I could."

"I get that. My sister is a decade older than me. We were never close. Too much difference in years. Plus, she and I are nothing alike. I get along well with my ex-brother-in-law, better than with her. He's hilarious! Too bad she divorced him. I would love to see him more often. He was more like a brother to me than she was a sister. She's a total diva and an extrovert. As we know, I'm neither of those. So, your sisters are married?"

"Yeah. They were married off instead of sent to college. Their husbands were already out of college and had started their careers. To me they seemed to be much older than my sisters, but I guess not really. Mom made them wait till they were twenty to get married, but the guys were like twenty-five and twenty-six, so it seemed huge to me. Dad made them get secretary and retail jobs to 'learn some work and life ethics' before they were sent to be housewives, because that's what *Dad* thought was best. I'm surprised he even let Mom work outside the house, come to think of it. He probably wouldn't have if she wasn't already working, and they didn't need the money so bad when we were kids."

I nod in silent agreement. My Spidey sense is going off with his parents. Something seems weird there. I'm going to research his story and see what I can find out about them. "Are your parents still alive?"

"Yeah. Still working, too. I don't think Dad will ever retire, but Mom's getting close. I check in on them every now and then, but not too much. I hold too much hatred for Dad. I probably shouldn't say that, but it's the truth. I find myself just wandering around the area and the house I grew up in looking for something, but I don't know what."

"And have you found any answers or clues?"

Looking back at me finally, he shakes his head. His eyes seem to cut right through me with their intensity. They are blazing green now, sending another shiver down my spine.

"Not sure what the questions are, so I don't think I've found any answers. I'm not even sure I know where to go for them. It's hard to be looking for something when you don't know what it is you're looking for. I mean, where do you even start? I feel so lost. You've given me a lot to think about. Thank you for that."

I smile sadly at him. He truly is a lost soul. I feel the need to make him whole so strongly. I want to give him the answers, but I don't know them either.

"Anytime. As you're here for me, I'm here for you. I'm going to research your life when I wake up. I'll see if I can find more questions for you to try to provoke something within your mind. I think you gave me a great base for the story though. We were completely different in our early years, but it feels like we were similar in more important ways. Maybe the character for our book should have multiple personalities, or be a set of identical twins to pull this off."

"Very funny. No, write it with your gut and use what stands out to you. Meld and mix us into a character as you see fit. You're the one with a psychology degree, along with all the rest of your fancy degrees. I saw them all hanging on your wall. I trust you to do this. I trust you fully with my life story. You already know more about me and how I feel than anyone else ever did. I wouldn't have told you if I didn't trust you, Gertie. No matter if I'm dead or not. I've never opened up to people. It's like no one cared enough to ask either, so I never talked."

Another foreign and strange feeling envelops my body. It feels like a full body hug filled with warmth.

"Thank you. That means a lot to me, Zeke. Not many people in my life, other than Quinn, ever sit and talk to me either. They don't take the time to really see me, let alone entrust me with such information. This is a first for me, too. It means a lot more than I know how to express."

Looking me straight in the eye, he smiles and nods.

A ringing noise starts in the distance and grows louder until I wake up to the bright light coming in through the blinds, I forgot to close, and I notice my phone ringing. Guess it is time to start another day.

Chapter 5

Zeke

Sitting at a table in the middle of a busy restaurant, it's my sisters' monthly lunch date and I've decided to crash it. Not that they'll know I'm here. I haven't checked in for years, but after my conversation with Gertie the other night, I decided it was time to see what I've been missing, if anything. They used to just chit chat about their husbands and never really seemed connected to each other, but it's been awhile.

Mandy, the older of my sisters, is sitting to my right drinking an ice tea while Abbey, the younger one, is sitting across from me drinking water. Looks like Abbey's pregnant again.

"How have you been feeling? Everything going ok so far this time around?" Mandy asks as she takes a drink.

Smiling, Abbey rolls her eyes. "Yeah. I really hoped we would've stopped at three but looks like number four decided for a surprise appearance. I hate being pregnant. I already told my doctor that he's tying my tubes after this one comes out. I mean, I love my children, but I'm tired of being a stay at home Mom. I want a job to get out of the house. Even just part-time. God Mandy, I go crazy sitting at home all day with them. At this rate, it'll be time for me to retire when the kids are finally out of the house."

Mandy laughs. "Yeah, I know what you mean. I hate that the guys won't let us get jobs or have a life outside the house during the day. Mom's lucky she got to keep hers."

Quiet reigns over the table, as the girls look at each other sadly.

Abbey sighs heavily. "Nah, I don't want Mom's life. At least my husband's faithful to me and loves me. He isn't just staying with me because of the kids, or because he doesn't want to be made a spectacle by getting a divorce. I mean, what century are we in? Why do they both feel that way? Ohhhh...let's worry about what everyone else thinks and be jerks to each other."

Mandy shakes her head. "I wouldn't have agreed to an arranged marriage like that to begin with. We did get lucky at least being able to pick our husbands. We're also lucky they're so good to us, even if they don't want us to work. I guess we should be more grateful. Eric does so much for me, but most importantly, he treats me and the kids well. He treats me as an equal instead of someone below him. He's cut back his hours to help more with the kids and to be a part of their activities. He doesn't push them into things like Dad did with Zeke and us. Eric still hates Dad for what he heard about Zeke's life. He wishes he could have gotten to know Zeke."

Abbey nods. "I really wish we could've known Zeke better, too. I mean, he was our brother. Maybe we could've helped him. Changed his life. I know he didn't die of natural causes; I don't care what they try to tell us. And honestly, if it would've been me, I probably would've done the same thing, only years sooner. I don't know how he dealt with all the shit Dad put him through. I feel horrible that he was carrying all that around and never talked to us. But then, we never really asked him about it either. I don't blame Mom at all for hating Dad. No wonder they don't talk anymore. Look what he caused their own child to do. I can't even think about losing a kid like that."

Looking like she's going to cry, Mandy's bottom lip starts quivering.

"Agreed. I hate Dad for that alone. I didn't even need to hear about the affairs and everything else. I mean, I'm glad Mom sat us down after losing Zeke to explain 'their life', or lack thereof, and come clean, but still. She needs to just leave him and try to be happy, but just like everyone else, he's running her life too. I'm just glad that you and I are out from under his thumb. I would much rather have Eric trying to run my life than Dad. I can side track Eric and get my way with him. That's why I don't fight the whole job thing too much. He gives in on so many other things that it's just not worth it for me to push too much. I've learned to pick my battles. But then, I only have two kids, and they're getting old enough to take care of themselves."

Abbey laughs. "Yeah. Maybe I'll feel that way when mine are eight and twelve. Mike just needs to let me have something. I keep asking about a part-time at home job, like on the computer or something. He's 'thinking about it'.

But I see your point, Mike and Eric are much better than Dad. They are way above Dad. At least their parents welcomed us in and treat us like their own. We finally have true parental interaction. And our kids have grandparents that are normal on one side of the family."

"True. So, tell me about your last doctor's appointment?"

At this point, I find myself back at my bench not needing to hear the gory details of a baby doctor appointment. I never knew any of that stuff about my parents or my sisters' husbands. Feeling relieved that they're happy, and have husbands that are trying their best to treat them well and who love and care for them, I'm nowhere as worried about them as I had been.

Seeing for myself that they know love and have good lives, I sigh with contentment. It feels like I've released some heavy weight from my shoulders, like an answer has been granted to me. We were never close, but they're still my little sisters. I always felt the 'family first' with them. We were all in that crappy situation. I feel the need to look after them, even now.

I do feel guilty that they think they could have helped me. Everyone seems to have that thought after a family member's death. I wonder if I was too good of an actor at keeping everything in? What would have happened if I at least let someone know how I felt? Maybe I should've let some of it show so people would've asked. Would the world have stopped? No. Wait, why was it their responsibility to ask me?

Why couldn't I just open up? Was I too weak of a person? No, I don't think that was it. I felt pretty strong emotionally, for the most part. It wasn't like anyone, other than my Dad, really did anything wrong to me. I did stick up for myself with others and teammates. I was the one who built the walls so no one could get inside. I was the one who pushed people away or kept them at arm's length. Basically, I was the one who let my Dad walk all over me. I have no one to blame but myself. Huh. Well isn't that a kick in the pants.

Crap. Looks like I did cause all the pain myself. Did I cause myself to be in all that emotional pain and turmoil? Yep. I did, and I don't like that at all. I didn't have to allow my Dad to push me into things I didn't want to do as an adult. No, he was definitely not a good parent, the worst actually, but once I got to a certain age I should've started pushing back and taking over my own life. There was no reason to just let him walk all over me.

Standing up, I start pacing. I really don't like the thought that I was the cause of my own unhappiness, but I really was. I mean, I was the one that made my choices. Yeah, he pushed me in certain directions and made me feel like I didn't have a choice, but ultimately, I did. I think deep down I knew I did, but I didn't want to cause waves in the family. I hated confrontation. I think I liked the idea that if things went wrong, I could blame him and not admit it was something that I did.

Was I really that way? Did I feel the need to be perfect?

I never felt like I did, but I guess, maybe? Did I choose to believe that I had to be perfect, and if I wasn't then I wasn't good enough for my family? I did always feel like I didn't belong. Was this my way of trying to fit in? To try to prove my worth?

Well crap. I think it was. Doesn't that just suck eggs.

Chapter 6

Gertie

Spending the afternoon researching Zeke, I'm finding some amazing articles. He was an amazing athlete, and if this is what he accomplished while not really caring, I can only imagine what he could've done if he enjoyed it and tried. I find multiple photos of him on his roommate's social media pages.

It looks like Roman had a hard time with Zeke's death. He posted a lot of photos of them together around the time Zeke died. Zeke described himself pretty well. I could tell exactly which one he was right away. Roman is a couple inches taller than Zeke and slightly darker skin.

Roman's pages seem full of remorse. His posts are sad, kind of depressing. He works at the same hospital and is now a resident there in some kind of supervisory position. It's a big long title that means nothing to me, but he looks proud in the photo with the announcement of his promotion. I want to ask Zeke if that's still the same apartment. I don't think I could stay there if a good friend and roommate died in it. Isn't that a little morbid? Ok, maybe not to others. Who knows?

Finding his sisters was easy, and I began stalking them on social media. They all look a lot alike. None of them out grew their baby faces and freckles. His nieces and nephews all look like him. I wonder if he knows that? I have this urge to call out to him and show him, but he probably already knows.

The photos of his parents explain a lot. I feel like there's a back story that would be good to know, but there is no way I'm contacting those people. Looking at the photos, I pick up their energy and it's not good. Instantly they make me think of a couple that stayed married for the kids, and then stayed married because they didn't want others to think badly about them with a divorce. It feels like they care too much about what others think of them. Maybe that's why his Dad let his Mom continue working? Yeah, Spidey sense tells me yes on that one. Feeling that they don't love each other, I wonder if they ever did. Arranged marriage maybe? Did people still do that back then?

Soaking in all the information I can over the afternoon, I start writing out notes and timelines. I have a basic plot line down on paper with the rest floating around in my head, but there are some big holes that I still need to fill. I make notes of those too, so I can start brainstorming them at a later point. Feeling excited about everything I got accomplished, I decide to cook supper. I'm craving spaghetti and Quinn loves meatballs. Walking to the store, I grab the needed things and start in on supper.

"Are you seriously cooking and singing? And not just singing, but singing 'Faith' by George Michael? You hate that song! What's going on with you?"

Looking over my shoulder, I see Quinn's face. Pure, unadulterated horror. He knows I've hated this song since high school for the stupidest reason. Why would a normal person hate a song because the boy they were crushing on had a girlfriend and her name was Faith? Maybe because said boy would go through the halls singing the song? I'm a screwed-up individual to hold on to that for all these years. Quinn also knows that I never cook, because I have a weird OCD thing about feeling the texture of some foods, especially raw meat, on my hands.

"Yes, to both, my love. I'm cooking spaghetti and meatballs and before you say anything, the meatballs were purchased premade. You know I can't touch them. Freaks me the hell out." I shiver at the thought as my stomach rolls. Yuck.

"I've never understood that. You're the granddaughter of a butcher. You used to cut meat and grind it all the time when you were young! I know, because I was there and watched you. How can you not touch it now? And also, yum. Thank you. What's the occasion?"

"I don't understand it, either. The older I get, the more OCD I get about certain things. Just feeling the meat squish between my fingers sends me into a panic attack. Thank the grocery store's deli department for those. And I was kind of hungry and craving spaghetti. I know you like the meatballs, so I grabbed them for you. Boiling water and breaking pasta doesn't freak me out, and neither does spaghetti sauce from a jar. I'm all good there. Set the table, would you?"

Continuing to stare at me like I've been taken over by an alien, he cocks his head to the side while contemplating the whole scenario. "You left the apartment and went to the store? Did you walk? How's your leg and ankle?"

"I did. It's only a half a mile away and all on safe streets. Ankle hurts a little but leg's fine. I've been house bound and in need of a break. Plus, walking helped clear my head. I miss my walks down by the creek. They have such a calming effect on me, but I knew I wouldn't make it that far today, so I did what I could. I feel like I was going to go crazy in here." I look around our kitchen. I do love this place but sometimes too much of it drives me a little stir crazy.

"Yeah I get that. We're hermits, but it's by choice. It's totally different when you can't leave. So, why'd you need your head cleared? Something going on that I don't know about?"

Pausing a second from stirring the sauce, I ponder what to tell Quinn. Do I want to tell him about Zeke, yet? He's going to think I'm batshit crazy. Quinn doesn't believe in the afterlife or ghosts, or does he? It's not a topic that ever came up between us that I can remember. He'll most likely take me to the ER for head problems if I tell him. I improvise.

"I decided to finally sit down and write a book. I still have PTO from the accident, and the money I'm getting from the insurance company to 'settle up' will keep me paid for about 3-4 years the way I live. So I decided that life is short, and I might as well give it a shot while I have the opportunity. Once I decided that, major plot bunnies were multiplying at alarming rates in my head. I needed to walk so I could sort through them and find one that I want to tackle first." Yeah, that sounds good and believable. Go me.

Staring at me with his head tilted to the side, Quinn looks like he doesn't quite believe me, but he eventually nods. "That's great! I'm glad you finally decided to dive in. You're going to rock a novel. Your short stories are perfection, whether you think so or not. About time you jump that fence. So, which bunny won? Whatcha writing?" His eyes sparkle in delight, like we're plotting some big secret or joke. I can't help but laugh at him.

"I think it may kinda be based on me, but more dramatized. He'll get a happy ever after... probably, even if I never do. I decided to make the character male and incorporate stories from other's lives too. His background will be somewhat like mine and his personality will probably be like mine. I think it'll be easier to write for my first main character. And who knows? Maybe by getting him a life, I can get one of my own?"

I look everywhere but at Quinn as I talk, because I don't want him to be able to see right through me. He knows me better than I know myself. I can't lie to him or withhold the truth. This won't be easy. Maybe I should just bite the bullet and explain Zeke to him? Maybe.... but some other day. Yep, I'm Queen of procrastination for anything uncomfortable; let me rule over my kingdom in peace, please.

"But who knows, it may take a turn and go into a whole other direction and story. I won't fully know until I sit down and start it, you know?"

Nodding, Quinn sets the table. He's biting his lip like he does when he's thinking. "Do I get to help at all? You know I like to help you brainstorm."

"Of course! First thing I need are names, fictional town name and things like that. Should I get paper and we could do that over supper?" The more I include Quinn now, the easier the withholding the Zeke information will be. Keep him included and he'll be distracted and happy.

"Oh! I'll get some rum and cokes for us. Brainstorming's always better with alcohol! Opens up the creative juices."

Placing the food on the table, we dig in. The rest of our night is spent brain storming, drinking, and laughing until we fall asleep on the couch with pieces of paper, full of ideas, everywhere in the living room.

Chapter 7

Zeke

I'm sitting on the bench daydreaming when Gertie falls down beside him. "Hey good looking? What's happening?"

I laugh at her slurred words. "Uh, a little drunk, are you?"

Gertie laughs like I've never heard her before. It sounds genuine and strong. "I guess so. Quinn and I had dinner and watched... uh, something and drank. I don't drink. Not normally. Were we celebrating? Uh...yeah, why were we drinking?"

Her face looks more relaxed than I've seen thus far. Shaking my head at her slurring words and the confused look on her face, I respond, "I've no clue why you were drinking. But I'm curious why you came here in your drunken dream stupor."

She looks at me like she's trying to solve world hunger. "I've no idea. You seem to be on my mind all the time. I think I missed you. But, uh, I've never really missed anyone before, so, uh...maybe?"

I can't tell if she's being serious or not. "What do you mean you haven't missed people before? What about your family and Quinn?"

Looking away from me, she tries to remain upright on the bench. "I've missed them when they go away, but not like this. Lately...I just want to hang here with you. It's so peaceful. There're no people. Energy is good. And you're hot. Not in temperature. I wouldn't know that. I can't touch you. I wanna, but I can't."

Well, there's something I didn't know. "Thank you. You aren't too bad yourself."

Gertie makes a noise that I think is supposed to be a tsk'ing sound, but sounds more like an animal farting. "I'm bad. I'm chubby. I'm a wallflower that blends in. I don't get second looks from people because I'm boring. No one wants someone like me. That's why I stopped trying to find anyone. They all think they're better than me or 'deserve' better than me. I don't need'em anyway. I'm happy just as I am."

Turning to look at her, I sense she's lying. "Are you happy Gertie? Seriously and totally happy and fulfilled?"

I know the answer to this, but she needs to acknowledge it. You can tell by looking at her that she isn't at all happy with her life. It's written all over her face, but not in a way that makes her ugly. She's so beautiful in her simplicity. Her blue eyes are striking against her pale and slightly freckled face with her dark brown, slightly wavy hair and purple bangs. I'm sure that people have noticed her but tended to ignore her because of the 'vibe' she gives off.

Surprising me by looking me straight in the eye for a moment, she quickly looks away. "Of course, why wouldn't I be?"

"Gertie, Look at me."

Continuing to look out over the waterfall, she tries to ignore me as I stare at the side of her face. I'll win this stare down. This is too important not to have eye contact for. As I stare, I take in all of her. She is what others may call chubby, but in a proportional way that makes her adorable. She would probably hit me for saying that, but I really like the way she looks. She has full breasts and hips. Heavier thighs than most woman, but they all blend together well. She is short, but would fit perfectly up against my body.

I really wish I could give her a hug and just feel her against me. I crave the ability to touch her, put my arm around her, grab her hand...anything. Affection was something I never had in my lifetime, and something she's never had in hers. It's killing me not to touch her. Huh, never notice how much you use a 'turn of phrase' until it doesn't make sense in your current situation.

Gertie finally looks over at me with a big sigh. "What Zeke?"

"A couple things. First, don't lie to me again. I know you know you're not happy. Just admit it. There's no harm in admitting something like that. It's the first step to solving the problem and making changes to your life. Plus, you told me earlier in previous conversations that you aren't happy. Don't mask it. That's a reflex you do. Stop it, now. Second, you and only you can make yourself happy, Gertie. Don't rely on anyone else. If you want to be happy, that's your choice to make. If you do choose it, then you need to make the changes to get there. Choose happy Gertie, please, not this current stagnant state you're in. Make it so. Third, you're not boring. To me, you're everything but boring. You make me laugh. You understand me. You listen to me. You're beautiful. You need to learn to own that crap and stop being such a mopey wallflower. You're the one making yourself feel that way."

Seeing her gear up to fight back, I stop and hold my hand up. "No, this is the time for me to say my piece. Whether you'll remember it, I don't know, but it needs said. I sit here and worry about you Gertie. You've walled yourself up so much that you're deliberately keeping people out. You're pushing them away on purpose. You know how I know that? Because I did the exact same thing. You've turned yourself into a hermit when you don't have to be one. You don't go out and socialize. These are choices that you've made. Then you sit here and blame others for not choosing you. You're wrong about that. You don't give people a chance. I did the same thing in my life. Look where it got me. I ended up killing myself to finally have peace and freedom from the heck that was behind my self-built walls. Don't be like me. You have time to change, Gertie. I didn't. This type of life hurts. It's depressing. You need to be more than that. You deserve to be more than that."

Looking away from me, she crosses her arms. Yeah, she's mad at me, but tough. I need to get this through her head. "Gertie. Listen to me. I've learned many things about myself and my life since I met you. You helped me reconcile why I was the way I was, and why I did what I did. You provoked me to look at the people in my life, and that made me realize a lot of things I didn't see then. Everything that happened in my life, to me, was because of choices that I, and I alone, made. Or really, it was my lack of choices. Most of the time I just let life go on around me and did nothing at all, which in turn, is a choice. Please don't do that to yourself. Loosen up a little bit. Try to change even a few small things and chose happy."

Taking a deep breath, she lets it out in a long sigh while rubbing her eyes. "Zeke, how the hell am I supposed to choose to be happy when the only person, the only thing that I want...and that I know would make me happy, is you? To be here with you. Shit, to be anywhere with you. Yeah, I know we haven't known each other long. But seriously, that's how I feel."

Her arms fall to her sides like she's giving up. "You soothe my inner craziness…the voices that tell me how yucky I am. You calm the energy around me. You're the first person…thing…soul, whatever, that I feel completely comfortable to be around, even more so than Quinn. So how? Tell me. Because I can't figure it out. I've got no one to talk to about this except you. And I refuse to talk to you about it because, well, it's awkward and I don't like that. I don't like change. I don't like feelings. I don't do uncomfortable. All of this is new and confusing to me, and I don't know how to deal with it all. So, how do I do it hot shot? How do I deal with any of this? How do I stop building and reinforcing the walls? I don't have a clue when I'm doing it, or how I even do it? It just happens! I don't do it on purpose."

Screaming at me now, her frustration level is high; I can feel her shaking beside me. "Gertie, you did just talk to me about it, and the world didn't end."

While rubbing her eyes and taking deep breaths, I know she's trying to calm down.

"Yeah, only took how many glasses of whatever Quinn and I were drinking to shut down my filter so something could slip out."

"Gertie, seriously. After all the conversations we've had, and all the things I've told you about myself, I can't believe that you don't feel like you can talk to me about this. You can talk to me about anything, heck, everything. I love our conversations. I could literally sit and listen to you and talk with you for hours without getting bored. How's that possible? I've never met anyone like you before. I never could've done that with anyone in my life. Not even Roman. You are fun and adorable, and I feel totally at ease with you. I've never said that about anyone else. You're unique, in a great way. I can't understand why you don't realize it."

Exhaustion is clearly setting in as she lays her head back on the bench, but flashes a smile over at me. The light in her eyes is twinkling again, finally. "Adorable? Really? You need eye glasses up here, dude."

Dropping my head back, I sigh. This girl is going to drive me crazy. "Gert, when are you going to realize that you're not an ugly duckling? For the love of everything holy, you're adorable, and I stand by my eyesight. Can you please take the darn compliment, accept it, own it, and go on? Please? For me." She chuckles at my exasperation.

"I can't guarantee anything, but I'll try. I'm serious Zeke, I have no clue how to change. I don't know where to start, and honestly, I don't know if I'm ready or willing to. I'm settled into my life and comfortable for now."

I was afraid of that.

Lacie Minier

Chapter 8

Gertie

Waking up with a hellish hangover and neck pain, I see stinking, huge feet in my face, and a cat's ass on my forehead. "What the hell? Why am I not in my bed?" I move my foot slightly and end up kicking Quinn in the head.

"Motherfucker! What'd you do that for?" Quinn slaps at my feet.

Oh, this will be a wonderful morning, both of us hungover and grouchy.

"Quinn, you're squishing the hell out of me. Get up, you lug. I've got to pee, your knee is on my bladder, and I can't move. You've got me pinned down. So unless you want to clean piss out of the couch, move your sorry ass NOW."

"Jesus. Keep your pants on." Moving slightly back, he falls off the couch.

I can't stop laughing. "Oh shit, I really have to pee now." Jumping over his body as he lays there in shock, I hear him mutter a blue streak of profanity. One thing I love about Quinn is his ability to string curse words together like a sailor on leave. It never ceases to crack me up and amaze me at the rawness of his imagination.

After relieving my bladder, brushing my teeth, and pulling my hair into my signature messy bun, I change my clothes, and go in search of the coffee that I suddenly smell. Quinn, thankfully, has a pot almost finished and is looking more human, also. "Do you want me to take you to your check-up today, or are you going by yourself? I know you're cleared to drive now."

"Oh, if you're not busy then yeah, come along. We could go to dinner afterwards. I need to get out of here for a little while. I'm going stir crazy. How do you feel about Red Robin?"

"Sounds good. My schedule's clear for the next couple days so let's do this. Shopping at Target, too? We could use some stuff for the apartment."

"Oh…you had me at Target! Yep! You're driving, and you're buying supper. I cooked last night." Winking at him, I head back to my room to relax for a while. I had a dream with Zeke last night, and I don't remember it. I don't feel like it was anything about the book, but I wish I could remember what we talked about. Something makes me feel like it was important.

"Zeke, you out there? What am I forgetting from our conversation last night during my drunken stupor?"

I often feel stupid talking to the air, but usually I get some kind of answer. This morning I wait and get nothing. No smells. No sense of him being around. I really can't remember the dream, but I have that feeling of warmth I get after waking up from spending my dream time with him. Never in my life did I expect to have that "warm and fuzzy" feeling people talk about, but that's the only way to describe it. It feels like I'm blanketed in a warm cocoon. Geez, I'm turning into a sap.

Arriving at my doctor's appointment hours later, I check in while Quinn goes in search of seats. The waiting room's packed with screaming kids running all over the place. I don't much like kids. Their energy is too strong for me to handle. I also don't like people in my personal bubble. I'm not going to get my way in here today. Quinn grabs the last two seats that I can see, and thankfully, leaves me the one between him and the aisle. Sitting down, I take some deep breathes. Seriously, they need a special section for people with social anxiety. This is overwhelming my senses. My heart is racing and I'm breaking out in sweats. Too much energy from people who aren't positive. Too many hectic thoughts that I can feel and hear. Ug!

Sitting here trying to keep calm, I pull out my phone and make it look like I'm deeply enthralled with it, so I can block out and ignore the other people in the waiting room. Quinn's biting his finger nails, like usual in public, and his leg's bouncing. Looking up to tell him to stop, I accidentally make eye contact with the lady across from me.

"Oh sweetie, you have the most beautiful purple bangs! I love that color! Too bad they don't match the rest of your hair." She says as she scrunches her nose up at me.

Quinn stills and the rest of the waiting room goes quiet. As one, we all look at her like she's an alien. A rude alien, who has completely pale skin and badly dyed black hair. Ok. Did *this* lady just say that to me? In front of about thirty people? What the hell's wrong with people? And why did the kids even go silent? Creepy.

Looking over at Quinn to see if it's just me, I see his mouth hanging open. Neither of us has anything to say. Shaking my head, I look back down at my phone as the noise resumes around us. A text comes up on my phone.

Quinn: *Did that bitch with the horrid hair really just say that to you? I mean, seriously?*

Me: *yep. I hate people.*

Quinn: *exactly. I mean, WTF?*

Resuming my Facebook scanning, I ignore everyone. Looking at happy little dogs on Facebook always calms me down. What seems like an hour later, but was probably only about ten minutes, I get called. Thankfully, the doctor thinks everything looks good and is healing nicely. I'm cleared to go back to normal activities, including my daily walks. He sends me off to the lab for one last bloodwork.

As I'm sitting in the hallway waiting to be taken back for the vampires to attack my veins, I continue scrolling through anything on my phone to look occupied. An old man pushes a female skeleton with skin up in a wheelchair and parks her right next to me.

"I'll be back in a minute; watch her for me." He says before walking away.

Scanning around to see who he's talking to, it becomes apparent that it's me. There's no one else in this secluded hallway but us. Looking over at the skeleton with skin, I involuntarily cringe. A shiver goes straight down my spine. She literally looks dead but with better color. Looking away from her, because she seriously gives me a case of the creeps, I go back to my phone.

Then I feel it. She's petting my hair. The skeleton, who has to be at least a hundred years old, is touching me and petting my hair. I feel my heart race and panic starts to claim me. Breathing is getting ragged and twitching is occurring. When I mistakenly glance at her, she starts muttering in German to me. I have absolutely no clue what she's saying. And why is she petting my hair?

Contemplating how rude it would be to move a couple seats down and leave her by herself, she grabs a handful of my hair. She's visibly becoming frustrated that I'm not understanding her. She's pulling my hair violently for someone who looks like she has no muscle mass. Seriously, why do these things happen to me? How do I get out of this? OUCH!

Starting to shake, I almost can't breathe at all now. Struggling to get away with my hair still on my head, I stand. Immediately after, the man comes back, nods thanks, and pushes her away. Why couldn't he have shown up before I got away on my own? Sitting back down, I automatically put my head between my legs. Deep breathing, that's what I need. The nurse choses that moment to come out and call my name for bloodwork. Thank the freaking heavens. Noticing my panic, she rubs my back and helps me slow my breathing. God love her, she is the sweetest thing.

As soon as my blood's in the test tube, I get the hell out of Dodge before anything else happens. I mean, I can only take so much social interaction to begin with, but these things are enough to send me into hermitville for a month, minimum. But wait… For some reason, isolating myself seems wrong, but it's never bugged me before.

Again, *why the hell was she petting me*? That part really freaks me out. I can't get past it. Every time I think about it I shudder.

Getting into the car, I tell Quinn what the doctor said and about female skeletor, the toucher. Of course, Quinn finds it hilarious, but only because it didn't happen to him. My body is still quaking with shivers down my spine and my hair feels as if it's standing on end. We decide on a drive-thru dinner instead of Red Robin and head home. I've had enough peopling for one day; I need my Freddie, and the sanctuary of home.

After supper and a long, hot bath, I crawl into my oversized beanbag with my laptop to write and research more of Zeke's story. I stare at a blank document for a while and listen to some music. At some point I fall asleep, and am rewarded with another dream with Zeke in it.

"So, you had a big day today. Panic much?" Zeke asks while laughing. Once again, we're sitting on our spot on the bench surrounded by the beauty of the flowers and waterfall. Just sitting in this place with him instantly makes me breathe easier and I feel better. A calmness settles over me.

"Why can't I just live here? I could bring an air mattress and stay in this peace forever."

"Because when you come here and stay then you've died. You're not ready to be here permanently, yet. You have something to accomplish first, remember? Do you ever listen to me?" He shakes his head in frustration. Is it wrong that I like to push his buttons?

I can't help but smile. "Yeah, I do. But I don't always like what you say. Can't you give me good news for once? And why didn't you help with female skeletor?"

Zeke smirks. "I can't help every time. You still have lessons to learn and overcome. She was no real threat to you. I just stood by and watched."

"Oh thanks. She freaking grabbed and pulled my hair! How's that no threat? She could have made me bald!"

"Oh, get over it already. Ok, so what are we talking about tonight? Apparently, you need more ideas since you fell asleep trying to write. Am I that boring to you?"

"I thought angels were supposed to be nice and supportive? And help you with hair grabbing skeletors!"

"Oh my gosh. I'm not an angel. You really don't listen to me, do you? We. Have. Been. Through. This." Zeke says between his gritted teeth. His eyes brighten in their intensity and his hand ball together.

Laughter creeps out again, he really is funny. "Wow, apparently you aren't since you're getting bitey. Ok cowboy, calm down. I'm just teasing you. I know you're a 'lost soul' looking for your way. I don't understand why you get so annoyed when I call you an angel. Do I hit a nerve? Who knows, you just may end up being my angel in the long run. Now, tell me more about what a little devil you were when you were alive. I need to formulate some words here, but first I have to understand why you don't think you are an angel, because really, I want to know."

Zeke looks away; I've noticed he does that when he goes deep into thought. He leans forward with his elbows on his legs and his head in his hands. We're quiet for a couple of minutes until he finally looks up, and as he stares straight ahead, he responds, "I'm no angel. I wasn't an angel in life, and I won't be here either. I mean, I killed myself. That is definitely not angel material. I'm still screwed up. When I was alive, I looked past a lot of things that happened around me that I should have spoken up about, but didn't, because I didn't want to call attention to myself. People got bullied, emotionally and verbally hurt in front of me, and I did nothing. I walked away and pretended nothing happened. That's not right. I'll always feel guilty about that. I don't want to mislead you or anyone else."

I nod. "I get it. I'm sorry that I teased you. But, you have to know that you're a good soul, deep down, if you're here and 'assigned' to help me. *They*, whoever *they* are, wouldn't appoint someone bad or 'screwed up' to help others. There's something about you that needs redeemed. You're not as bad as you think you are. Snap out of it. Talk. I don't care about what. If you need to get rid of some of your guilt about the bullies, try telling me stories about what happened. But talk to me. It's the only way you'll feel better."

Glancing over his shoulder, he stares deep into my eyes. His intensity makes me feel like he is looking deep into my soul. I start to feel uncomfortable, again, as those damned butterflies party up a storm. Smirking at me, he shakes his head. "You, Gertie, are much smarter than you give yourself credit for. Ok, I see where you're going with this, and I guess you've got a point. But the bullies are for another time. Did you do any research on me?"

"I did. I'm a good little writer. Ok, so you told me all the basics last time, and I was able to verify them so I could make sure I had the right person. You didn't look anything like you do now. You're right, you had such a cute baby face." I reach over to try to pinch his face but feel nothing but warm air. Smirking back at him, I know I'm going to drive him crazy.

Is this flirting? Am I actually flirting with someone? Well holy shit. I think I may be. Isn't that something?

"You're such a pain in the butt, you know that, right?"

Laughing, I shrug and continue. "I try. Your sisters are both still married and home with their kids. They do look happy by their social media posts though. And I saw a ton of articles about your games and awards in the sports realm. There were even articles about how well you did your job after college; the one you hated. Your fellow teammates and clients seemed to really like and admire you. From your appearance, there was no sign of depression or anything else that would have led to suicide. I can see how you pulled it off."

"Yeah. I became the king of fake smiles and fake happiness."

"You even did it without drugs or alcohol. That's scarily impressive."

Zeke nods. "I hated the taste of alcohol. And I was afraid that if I took anything or drank, I'd start talking and everyone would learn my secrets. Or I would tell Dad off and cause family problems. So, I stayed sober to keep control and wallowed in hate for myself and others. I lived my life feeling like a coward, because I wouldn't push myself to stand up to Dad. Sad, isn't it?"

"No. Not sad. You're a peacekeeper, or tried to be. That isn't bad. Bad for you, but not your family. Most people can't pull it off, but you did. Unfortunately, it ended up taking a major toll on you. There was no balance since you didn't know how to be yourself. Because your Dad never allowed you to find out who you were, and dictated your whole life, he kept your whole family from knowing you, too. Your friend's families seemed to be the same way, so it was all you knew growing up. That's your parent's fault, not yours. You were never taught how to figure out who you truly are. They didn't even show you how once you were an adult. But now's your chance. Did you get anywhere with the questions I asked you last time: Why did you go back into human form last time? What were you on earth to learn?"

I have a feeling Zeke still doesn't know, but I figure the more I push him, the closer he'll come to finding the answer.

"I don't know. I did think about it. Even went back home and wandered around. Thought about a lot of things that happened trying to get some perspective. I visited my sisters and learned a lot of crap I didn't know about my parents, but I also saw that they're both happy, so that helped me relieve some guilt and worry. I feel like this isn't the only life where I was a 'pushover' and constantly at a loss. It feels like I came back to look for something; I feel like I've always struggled in life to find out who I am. Maybe I've gone centuries looking for the true me, or maybe it's my other half, or something… Something feels like it's missing and always has been. I just can't narrow down exactly what that is."

Nodding to him, I feel a deep ping in my chest. All of what he's saying is how I've always felt. Feeling empty and lost, always searching and full of confusion. Frustration on top of frustration.

"I know that feeling extremely well; Quinn and I talk about it a lot. We feel like soul mates on some levels, but not on all of them. It's like we fill a certain hole within each other, but there's still a bigger hole in both of us where something's missing. We feel like we're constantly searching for that missing piece. That's probably why I have so many degrees and keep going back for more education. To find that missing piece."

"Exactly! Although, I've never had a Quinn. My roommate came close. Roman's the one who knew me the best, but even you know more than he did. He knew all the basics and safe things: my favorite foods, colors, TV shows, and movies. You know, those types of things that didn't really mean crap. They weren't a real indicator of who I truly was. They constantly changed as I got older. But you, you know my deep thoughts and secrets. I've told you what I was thinking and feeling. I give you the gold and show you my heart. He didn't even know that I died without ever having sex. No one tempted me enough. I was always afraid of getting too close to someone, and no one ever tried to break through, anyway. I never even had urges, so I think maybe I was asexual."

"That's what Quinn says too. Although, in college he went through a drunken year where he tried everyone, no matter gender, just to see if he could figure himself out. He claims he found no answers and became celibate instead. For me, sex means nothing without finding that one soul who completes me without question. One who accepts me for who I am, quirks and all. They'd have to accept that I'm a complete fruit loop who has panic attacks, that I look too deeply into everything, that the only horror movies I like are a mind-fuck Hitchcock style movie, that I love stupid funny movies, and that I may want to listen to music and read while not paying attention to them at all some nights. They'd need to understand that I need free time to be alone and just breathe. They'd have to accept Freddie and Quinn, because they're such big parts of my life and always will be. They'd have to accept my secret tie-dye addiction, my oversized beanbag chair, and what Quinn refers to as my constant state of 'college girl' dress and décor. You know what I mean? If they can't, well see ya later. I don't have time for you."

Zeke nods. "Totally get that. Those things are who you are once they've been around longer than a few years. Those are outwards projections of yourself and your personality. Does it bother you? Quinn being asexual? Or what I told you about me? Do you see me in a different light now?"

I think about this for a minute. I know my answer needs to be perfect, because I can feel that he needs reassurance. Hey, when did I start to be able to feel his emotions? Well, this is new. Good, I can help better knowing what he's feeling.

"Not at all. Why should it? I believe that no one has the right to judge another person's feelings, thoughts, or sexuality for any reason. To reference the ever-popular phrase, Love is Love. There's a good reason for that saying, even if in our case, it's haven't been loved. But you know what I mean. In a world full of such negativity, why put more into it by telling someone they can't be positive and love someone because of gender or race? I never understood that. To be completely honest, there've been times that I've felt more masculine than feminine and wondered if I wasn't meant to be a male. I've never gone down that rabbit hole of thought completely; I won't allow myself, because in all honesty, who cares? I dress how I'm comfortable. I live how I want to. I really don't care what others think, and right now, I'm comfortable with the body I have, for the most part. I'd like smaller hips and thighs, but still. I know I sound ridiculous because of my social anxiety, but it's never brought on by the need for approval of others. My anxiety is brought on by their energy, not their thoughts toward me. The world is so full of negative energy; it's suffocating for me. Why do people add to negativity worrying about something that really is none of your business? If everyone just let people be happy, it would add more love and positivity to the world. OK, sorry, I really went out into left field on a tangent there. Did I TMI you?"

Zeke remains quiet for a few moments, almost too quiet. I start to wonder if I scared him with my brutal honesty. To be honest, I think I scared myself admitting all that out loud. Those thoughts have always floated around in my head, but most of the time I just let them be and don't poke at them too much. I don't really want to open doors and push myself to explore things that may or may not need to be resolved in this life. I figure if they do, then when the time's right, they'll be exposed. Sounds good, right? But seriously, I believe the universe is in charge, and will expose the thoughts I need to deal with at the right time. I have enough stress in life, why cause more?

"Yeah. I totally understand what you're saying. And it makes me feel even more comfortable with you. I mean, I've always felt weird since I'd never had the hormonal urges like the other guys. I would just nod in agreement and laugh when the locker room talk would start. They never knew that I had no clue what they were talking about. One girl I took to prom in high school told everyone afterwards that we 'like, totally did it', and I just let them think that and didn't contradict her. Why tell the truth when it helped me out in a way?"

"You totally shock me sometimes. Looking over all the articles I found about you, I'd never have guessed any of that. But, it does explain a lot about your psyche, and ultimately your suicide." Taking another deep breath, I feel a deep pain in my heart for Zeke. He went through so much without anyone's help. "I really wish we'd known each other when you were alive."

"Yeah, me too." Zeke sighs. "I could've really used a friend like you. It's so easy to talk to you. Especially now, knowing you're not judging me in any way. Heck, you didn't even laugh at me when I told you. I expected you to bust a gut."

"Am I that mean?"

He laughs, and those damned butterflies take flight again, and they seem to have brought some friends. My pulse is racing, but it feels like it's positive energy instead of panic. Huh. This is new. I can get behind this.

"No. I didn't mean it that way. But during my life, people tended to laugh at stuff like that. They looked down on people like me. The guys I hung around with would have. Roman may not have though. Heck, I'm not sure if he's straight, gay, or asexual. He was too busy with being pre-med, interning, and everything else. I barely saw him, and he had no time left to do anything else. That poor guy. He was a good guy, too. I was lucky to get paired up with him freshman year, and even luckier that he liked me enough to stick with me for all those years. He never probed or pushed for information. We hung out together when we had time and kept our friendship light. It was nice. I kind of miss him."

"I checked in on him on social media. He still seems just as busy. He's an ER doctor now and some type of supervisor. He has a long title behind his name that meant nothing to me. I can't imagine the stress he lives under. He seems like a nice guy, but no, no mention of a significant other of any sort."

"Huh." Mumbling, he returns to staring out in front of him. "Ok, well our time's almost over again. Any homework for me this time?"

"Ha! You do think I'm mean from making you do homework. I'd say keep trying to figure out what you were meant to learn, and why you came back. Try to find the answers for those questions, first. I'll see what I can think of, too. And for the love of everything holy, if some skeletor person tries to touch me again, STOP THEM!!"

Laughing a full belly laugh that I've never heard out of him before, he holds up his hands in surrender. "Yes Ma'am. Now go wake up, and take Freddie out before he pees on your bed."

I smile as I feel myself waking up. I open my eyes, and sure enough, I see Freddie staring down at me from my chest with hopeful eyes. "Come on boy, let's go for a walk."

Lacie Minier

Chapter 9

Gertie

Sitting on the couch petting Freddie, I'm staring into space. I dedicated today to writing, and again, nothing is coming. I have everything I need. Fully caffeinated coffee beside me, and my music is going through the Bluetooth. My laptop is on my lap and booted up to an open document. Now, why will my brain not work? I dropped Quinn off at the train station bright and early this morning so I've been awake. Now it's midafternoon, and with him away overnight, there's nothing here to distract me. Write damnit.

I stop petting Freddie and put my fingers to the keyboard. "Ok Zeke, what the hell? Why can't I write today? We made such progress the other day, and I have the whole first part of the book done. Why the block? Help me here, oh wise one."

His smell appears. I love that smell. Coffee and mocha. My two favorite things in the whole world, and they're his smell. Shutting my eyes, I take a deep breath. "OK, I know you're here. Help."

I keep my eyes closed thinking that maybe that'll help, and sitting back, I relax. My head falls on the back of the couch, and I put my feet up on the coffee table. Next thing I know, I'm sitting on the bench talking to him. "Wow, for the amount of caffeine pumping through my system, I shouldn't be asleep."

Chuckling, Zeke shakes his head. "You don't have to be asleep to talk to me. This is kind of a twilight state you're in. I guess you could call it a trance like state, or meditation. So, stop procrastinating. Why are you blocked?"

"To hell if I know. The words were flowing well the last couple of days since we last talked, and now I feel like I hit a wall."

"Well, let's see, you have my part for the story pretty much, right? From your research and what I've shared? I'm not sure what else I can tell you right now that would help. You do have to make up some stories to fill the book; I can't remember every little fight with my parents and such. Weren't you going to add part of you, too? Is that where you're at now?"

Staring out at the waterfall, I nod. Yep, that's exactly where I am. "Yeah."

Zeke silently sits and gazes at me. I can feel his eyes watching me until I finally turn my head to look at him. This is an annoying habit of his that I don't like. It makes me feel uncomfortable. I decide to give him light information to kill time.

"My name's Gertie Meyer, and I'm thirty-eight, single and totally fine with that. I'm dyslexic, introverted, and socially awkward. I also have anxiety and panic attacks. I'm a high empath who hates crowds and big groups of people. I'm just a big barrel of fun. Not. I live with Quinn in a three-bedroom apartment in the bottom of an old Victorian house in our small little town in Central PA. I have an emotional therapy dog named Freddie who keeps me sane, as much as possible. He's a brown and white Shih Tzu and my soul mate. Quinn has a gray long- haired cat named Petunia. Petunia and Freddie act like siblings. They secretly love each other, but don't like us to see them cuddle. It must go against some cat/dog code or something."

I look over at Zeke, he's giving me a look of confusion since this is not what he was talking about, but for me, right now, it's settling my nerves. So, I continue.

"Quinn and I come from two very different backgrounds but feel like we complete each other. We finish each other's sentences and know what the other is thinking without talking. I've an advantage since I can feel his emotions at any point I open myself up to him. He just knows me better than I know myself. I grew up in a 'Leave it to Beaver' type of family and home where we lived down the block from my Grandparents, and I have an older sister. My Mom worked in the family butcher business with my Grandpa, and my Dad was a factory worker. I was brought up in a Methodist church with an old-fashioned PA Dutch background. See, tons of fun and excitement."

Again, I stop and can't help the amusement I feel at the look of annoyance on Zeke's face. Apparently, I've made him speechless, so, again, I continue my nervous babble.

"Quinn, on the other hand, was brought up by his single Mom and Grandma in a two-bedroom apartment where he had to share a room with his Mom. She worked for the local pharmacy as a cashier, but never made enough money to get them out and a place of their own. He was basically raised by his Grandma who was a Woodstock reject. She never grew up and continued to dress the style and live the lifestyle. I loved that lady till her dying day. She was so much fun, but he was embarrassed by her all the time."

"Gertie, stop. That's what you decided to tell me? The surface stuff? Really?"

He looks intense. No dimple in sight, just bright green eyes staring at me like he's looking right through me. Or into me. He looks kind of intimidating since I feel like I know what he's looking for, and I don't feel like talking about it. I remain quiet.

"So, I've told you the majority of my life, and you researched the rest. I'm pretty much an open book at this point, yet I know nothing deep about you. A little one-sided, don't you think? How about you share something deeper now."

Looking away, my muscles tense, and I start to fidget. I can't seem to look at him while talking or thinking about this. "I don't want to. Don't you have some kind of powers that tell you what you need to know? Why should I have to tell you? You should already know." I can feel myself getting defensive, but I don't want to talk about myself. I've already told him more about me, and my thoughts, than anyone else. He knows things that even Quinn doesn't know. So why don't I feel comfortable enough to tell him more?

"Gertie. Seriously. After everything I've shared with you? You can't share some painful things with me? Some of your fears and feelings? Yeah, I may already know them, but I need to hear them from you, and you need to share them to feel better. Trust me, it works. I have more clarity, and less guilt now than I did before we started this journey. You know you have to do this. You can trust me. Let it out." By the time he was done talking his voice was so soft and caring that I let myself lean into his warmth.

Continuing to stare out at the waterfall, I'm unsure what I should say. I've never felt like there was much to my life, but apparently there's stuff that's really bugging me. I don't want to open up or visit those particular rabbit holes. Sighing heavily in frustration with this whole thing, I give in.

"Zeke. I don't know what to say. I feel like I have nothing to contribute. Who am I? Hell if I know. I'm a no one. That's who I am. I was a wallflower in school and happy to remain one. Yes, I made that choice, and I still stand behind it. I didn't want to be noticed. I didn't want attention. Both of which I still don't want. I did my own thing and stayed out of people's way. I had Quinn and my family. Actually, Quinn is my family. He's basically my non-biological twin brother. I'm thirty-eight years old and have accomplished nothing noteworthy. Thirty-eight years of nothing. Never been married, or in any kind of real relationship, because I find reasons why I don't like everyone. I can't trust people, because I see their true colors and faults immediately. I can't be around large groups of people without freaking out, because their combined energy becomes too overwhelming for me and sends me into panic attacks. I can't get close to people because I can see their soul and their true being through their energy, and see, or feel really, all their flaws. I'm a judgmental and picky person. I leave them alone, because I don't want to 'deal' with their flaws and attitudes. So, I sit alone with my dog and best friend, living a life that's lonely and stagnant."

By the time I'm done, I'm angry and rushing through the words. They're pouring out of me now at an alarming rate. I'm not sure where they're coming from, or why I'm so angry about them.

"I'm no one. I've put up so many walls to try to block being able to see true souls, so that I can have some kind of life and interact with people, and it doesn't work. No one gets through no matter what I do. I always find faults and back away. I barely leave the house anymore, unless I direly have to, because I can't handle the energy even just outside the house. There are people everywhere, even in this little podunk town. Hell, even the cows and farm animals around here have energy that I can sense and feel. And that isn't good either because they're on farms, and not in their natural habitat, and they know that. I can't handle it anymore. I need to live in a fucking bubble just to try to survive from day to day."

Taking a deep breath, I sigh and go on in a lower voice.

"I seriously just want to be normal, whatever normal is, and I never will be. I want to be able to handle life like everyone else. I can't. I just want to be loved, and to love someone other than family. And all these things taunt me, I'll never have any of them in this life. I know I won't. How do I know this, you ask? I have no fucking clue. It's something else I have no clue how to explain, but it's like I saw the future in a dream, and I just 'know' that I won't. Deep down in my bones and soul I know I can't. It's not a psycho mind game that I'm telling myself I won't, it's just a deep down knowing. A feeling that's there taunting me. It's a life's truth that I can't change. I'm apparently predestined to be alone and always take care of myself. I feel like this has been my life over and over again; it's like I'm stuck in a revolving door that won't let me out. Through many lifetimes, the same damned thing, over and over again."

Stopping to breathe again, I gather myself. I still can't look at Zeke but I know he's moved closer as I feel the warmth of his energy surrounding me.

"And is it too much to fucking ask to, for once, to have someone take care of me? To care for me? To actually love me and want to be with me? I mean, I take care of so many others. Quinn. The animals. My parents. I took care of my Grandparents. I've never minded; I've always enjoyed it. It gave me a purpose, but damn it! I'm tired, exhausted really. I've been strong for everyone else and use so much energy to just get through the damned day, every day. I just want someone to care for me. I want it to be about me for once."

Tearing up, I'm shaking at this point. I collapse into the side of the bench, and Zeke moves even closer to me so I can feel his energy again. He tries to put an arm around me, but it falls through me instead. He looks at me with sad eyes.

"I don't know or understand the whole feeling energy thing. That's something I never experienced in my life, but I completely understand the rest. I did the same thing in essence. I felt the same way. I lived to keep everyone else happy and never allowed myself to live for me. You don't know how to live for yourself either because of what life has dealt you. I never knew how to live for myself because I was never allowed to, or taught to. I was just shown what was expected of me and pushed that way. I went like a lamb to slaughter."

I see his point. "I really wish I could be normal, or at least live a semi-normal life. Go to the freaking grocery store without shaking and feeling overwhelmed." Noticing that there are tears rolling down my cheeks, I'm shocked by how I actually feel. I rarely allow myself to think too deeply on these things. I board them all up and stow them away in my head. I love not dealing with things. Confrontation and I aren't friends.

"I really want to hug you. We both need it. Neither of us had affection in our lives, and I think that would have helped me a lot. I know it would help you."

Nodding, I wish he could, too. "My parents hugged me and gave affection when I was younger. Quinn and I tend to cuddle on the couch, but it's not the same. It's not the same as what I assume it feels like to be hugged by someone who cares in a 'non-family' type of way. I've felt family type of love, but never romantic type of love and caring. I rarely thought much about it, but I guess this is something that I feel is missing, too. I always told myself that I was fine without it. I do feel like I'm destined to never have it. Too many barriers up against me. How do I let down the walls that protect me from others for one person? I mean, how do you even learn how to do that?"

Zeke shrugs his shoulders. "I don't know the answer to that, but I do know that your soul deserves and needs love. I believe that's the missing piece we both are striving and constantly looking for. We feel empty without it. That special person and piece to fill the holes within us. That person who knows us and understands us completely. Someone who doesn't just accept, but heck, enjoys our flaws. The person who cares, supports, and fights for us. I'm not sure either of us will ever have it. I feel like many lives ago I had it, but lost it somehow. I don't know how to explain it, but the longer I am up here and figuring out myself and my last life, I feel like more of other lives coming back to me. It's like it's right there, yet out of reach."

My heart hurts for him. Zeke deserves love and understanding so much. He's so kind and full of caring. He would make a wonderful partner for someone. He puts everyone else first. His flaws aren't even really flaws. They are pieces of himself that he misunderstood and is finally figuring out. He just needs some support and understanding. "You know Zeke, if you were still alive, I believe that you and I could be that person for each other. We sync. We get each other on levels that others don't. While I don't quite understand this instant trust we had in each other, we can't deny it's there. We've admitted that we've never felt this comfortable with others before."

Nodding, Zeke looks at me with sadness in his eyes. We sit in silence, encompassed in each other's energy and warmth. "So, do you know now where to take the story?"

Looking out over the waterfall, I figure out what had me stumped and where to take the book next. "I think so. But how do I write about something I've never felt? How do I give our character his happy ever after? How do I write love?"

"Who says it has to have a happy ending? Make it true to life. Write the pain and the emptiness he feels. Not that I think what I did was right, but it's a reality people need to face. Suicide happens and shouldn't be ignored. Maybe the character can't handle the world and ends it. Maybe he doesn't. Let him lead you to the answer on that one, but show the story in a light that makes it believable. Make it so the character's loveable and you're routing for them. Stories don't have to always have a happy ending. True life doesn't always have happy endings. We both know that. Maybe others need to know that this is 'normal' in life, also, and that they aren't different from others; they aren't alone in how they feel. Maybe that's the story we're meant to tell."

I ponder his words. Can I tell a realistic story and still make a difference in someone's life? Does anyone actually need to read it? Is it worth the time and effort even if no one reads it, or if they don't like it?

"Before you say what you're thinking out loud, no, it doesn't matter. I think this is more for us than anyone else. Write true to how you feel the story flows. Let our character tell you where his story goes. If by chance, it makes an impact on others, great. If not, well it made a difference to us. Be selfish. Do it for you and me. Don't worry about others. They don't matter."

Smiling, I start to feel lighter. "I hate that you can read my thoughts sometimes. Are you always in my head?"

"Nope. It's a scary place in there. I stay out of your head as much as I can. I only venture in when I see the wheels turning too much and feel your mood change." He flashes me his killer smile and that damn dimple. There goes the butterflies' party in my stomach again. "Yeah, I know you like the dimple."

"Knock it off! You're going to make me paranoid."

Laughing like a lunatic, he smiles even wider. "Good. Now, go be free and write."

"Yes Sir."

Lacie Minier

Chapter 10

Gertie

Waking up, I get to work. Ordering in Chinese so I don't have to take time out to cook, I write all through the night. I get any, and all thoughts that pop into my head down into the book or into my notes. Zeke's idea of writing it true to life works to open the flood gates. Although, I don't like that I broke down and opened up to him about my thoughts and feelings that I didn't even realize I had. But I do feel better after having those revelations and talking it all out with him. I know I can accept that I'm not going to be one of those people who have a happy ever after. He was right. Not everyone does. This is real life, not a freaking fairy tale. Not everything goes as planned here on earth. Not everyone gets everything they want. You just have to move on and keep going. I guess realization is part of the solution.

Saving the document, I close the laptop about five a.m. I take Freddie out for a quick walk and then ungracefully flop on the bed, falling right to sleep. I have a bunch of really weird dreams. Very vivid and real, the kind that feel like they are happening around me. Zeke's there in all of them, but he looks like he did in human form and acts like, what I assume, he acted like when he was alive. I see right through his mask and façade just like I do with everyone I meet in real life. He doesn't acknowledge me. I wonder if I'm just an observer and not a participant in the dreams.

Then the dream flips. I see him with Roman. They're just hanging out at home, and I have a bad feeling this is the night he takes his life. They're eating take out, and watching a movie. Zeke's heart feels heavy with sadness, but his outward appearance seems like he's fine. He's smiling and laughing at the movie. My heart hurts, and it feels like a lead ball tight in my chest. The phone rings and Roman's called in to work. He gets dressed and leaves for the night. Zeke turns off the movie and just sits there. I can hear his thoughts, and he's running the process of how to do it. I want to yell at him not to, but know I can't stop it. This isn't real, even though it feels like it is.

I watch as he goes to the fridge and pulls out the insulin. He grabs a needle from the cupboard and draws some up into the needle. He methodically puts the insulin back in the fridge and just stares at the needle on the counter. I can feel him going over and over it in his mind. The final thought is that he's just so lonely and feels so filled with guilt and frustration. He's so unhappy with his life. He feels like a coward and hates everything. He feels like nothing will ever get better, and he wouldn't even know how to go about making it better. He has no clue how to change his life or what he wants out of life other than to leave it.

He picks up the needle and delicately stabs himself in the stomach with it. He gently pushes the insulin into his body and caps the needle. He places it in the red container on the counter where Roman throws them away, and he walks the ten feet back to the couch and lays down. I know that within minutes it will be the end. I see a tear drop out of the corner of his eye, and he releases a long sigh. Turning my back, I walk out of the apartment.

Waking up suddenly, I'm confused as to where I am and what just happened. Freddie's still sleeping and curled up by my side snoring away, and Petunia's lying at my feet licking herself. Looking around the room, I slowly get my bearings. It was a dream. A very vivid dream. I had many of them this morning, but that one was like I was there and experienced it with Zeke. I felt the needle break his skin. I felt everything he felt and thought.

Zeke's smell surrounds me and I feel a blast of warmth. It grounds me and brings me back to the now. It wipes away all the fog in my head and the heaviness from my chest. Glancing at the clock, it reads noon. Slowly getting up, I head to the shower. Maybe the water will help get me moving today.

Chapter 11

Zeke

Sitting down hard on the shore of the waterfall, I try to relax. Geez. I hated running Gertie through the night of my suicide, but I knew it was something she needed to understand on a deeper level. I needed to re-experience it, also. Dang, that was hard to go through again. Especially now, going through it with Gertie. It ripped her apart and I could feel it. Every. Single. Moment. It hurt. Once she woke up, I went back to the scene to watch Roman come home and find me. I never knew how it affected him.

I feel guilty as heck now. I never knew anyone actually cared about me. Poor Roman. He's a doctor and saves lives for a living, and he came home to find his roommate dead on our couch. I stood there and watched him try CPR and to find something wrong with me. He couldn't help. I was long gone and already pretty cold by the time he got home. It felt like a dozen knives stabbing me in the heart to watch him break down and cry, right on my dead body's chest.

I can't look away. I didn't know that anyone cared about me enough to be upset by my death. I open myself up to feel his pain and thoughts, and they're filled with guilt. What does he have to feel guilt over? I watch him get out his cell and call for the coroner. I had to go; I couldn't experience anymore.

Sitting for what feels like hours, I can't get my mind off of Roman. Why guilt? I don't understand. There's something I'm missing. I haven't allowed myself to check in on him. I figured he would be busy with work and forget all about me easily. I assumed he'd moved on quickly. Maybe it's time to pay Roman a visit.

I'm not going to lie; I don't know exactly how this visit thing works. I don't do anything special; I just think it and Boom! I'm there. It's weird. No matter how long I'm 'here', wherever here is, I'm not going to get used to how things work. Since I thought about visiting Roman, I'm now standing in the middle of our apartment. I can't believe he's stayed here all these years, but it's a good location from the hospital and close to everything in the city.

Looking around, I notice that nothing's changed. Not one thing. Even the things that were mine are still here, not that I had much personal stuff. A couple of group pictures of the football and baseball teams I played on in college, a couple books I liked to read on the book case, and my dvd's are still in the cabinet. I walk back toward what was my bedroom and it's the same, also. All of my stuff is still here. Seven years later. What's going on? My bedroom looks just like it did the night I walked out of it for the last time. Nothing has dust on it though, so he must still clean it.

Hearing the door open, I walk into the hallway and see Roman, dressed in scrubs, coming in the apartment. He throws his keys in the dish by the door and his jacket over the chair. He looks like he has aged twenty years instead of seven. I guess being a doctor would do that. Long hours, right? Heck, I don't know. He grabs a bottled coffee drink from the frig and heads to the couch. He kicks his shoes off right by the coffee table and puts his feet up. His routine is exactly the same; the exact routine he had our freshman year when he would come home from anywhere, right down to the bottled beverage. That makes me smile. One thing I always liked about Roman was he was predictable.

Scanning the tv, he ends up with some music channel and lays his head back on the couch. Letting out a loud sigh, he looks like he's trying to relax. I walk around the couch and sit down on it. I want to talk to him but know I can't. He doesn't know I'm here and won't hear me. That frustrates the heck out of me. Since when can I feel frustrated? Apparently, as I progress *they* allow me more things? I need answers, and I can't get them if I can't talk to him. How am I supposed to do this? I watch him for a while until I realize that he's fallen asleep, so I sit back and think.

His cell phone rings and wakes him up, bringing my attention back to where I am. Looking down at it, he sighs again. Hits the button to answer it. "Hey dude, what's up?"

I listen intently hoping for some kind of helpful information.

"Nah, I'm not renting it out."

My room? Maybe?

"Yeah, I know that no one is living in it, but I don't want or need a roommate. I would rather be alone, but thanks for trying to help me out. I appreciate it."

Ok. That doesn't tell me much really.

"Nope. I can handle the payments myself. I'm a doctor you know. You're one of my nurses. I make the big bucks. Now stop worrying about me. I'm fine, really. I would be better if you would let me sleep. Aren't you the one who made me work six extra hours today?" he asked with a laugh in his tone.

Ok, maybe he is doing ok. Maybe? This doesn't feel right though. This whole apartment feels stale and stuck. It's heavy with sadness and something I can't seem to name.

"Yeah, Ok, see ya tomorrow."

Hanging up the phone, he turns off the TV and heads back to his room. It's still daylight, but he seems to be going to bed. I need to come back more often to gauge what's going on because something doesn't seem right. I need Gertie; she picks up on stuff like this all the time and could get me answers. Gertie! That's it. I need to find, or make, a way for her to get out here and visit Roman!

Gertie

The dream lingers with me all day. The smell of Zeke does, too. At this point, I can't tell if the smell is real or my imagination. I've noticed that the smell alone brings a calmness to me. Is my brain playing psychosomatic tricks on me? I just think I smell it to stay calm?

Going about my normal work and activities, I can't seem to shake the feeling of sadness I felt from Zeke right before waking up from the dream. I wanted to grab him and hold him and make it better. I've never felt like that before for someone, and I don't know what to do with that. What does that mean? I mean, I have wanted to help my family and friends and give them hugs, but this feeling was so much more intense. Like it was something that HAD to be done. Plus, while I hug my family, I don't do it willingly. I know I'm weird, but I don't like to be touched. Quinn gets a pass on that because of who he is to me, but otherwise, uh, no.

Quinn makes it home later that night and calls for me to pick him up at the train station. I zone out the whole way home in the car as he babbles on and on about his trip, and his new client. I don't understand what he's talking about when he goes into "work mode" since he has a fashion and decorating sense, and I live in tie dye, cotton, and fleece. He knows that I usually zone out and just listen for highlights, but apparently, I'm more out of it than normal. He, of course, notices and askes, "Hey, you ok? You look like you're in a world of your own."

"And that is different from any other day, how?"

"Haha. You're so funny. Like, more than normal or something. Your eyes are totally distant and you're sitting up right like you have a stick up your ass. What gives? Why are you so tense? Is everything ok?"

Silently chuckling to myself, I'm not even sure what I find funny. Man, I'm changing and don't even understand myself lately. "Yeah, everything's fine. I just had one of those really vivid dreams last night that has me all off today. You know the type, when you wake up and have no clue where or who you are? I can't seem to shake out of it, but everything's cool. Do you have to go back to this old dude's house again anytime soon?"

Quinn does his head tilt thing and looks me over silently for a minute, or two, and then continues with his run down of the new job he scored. I'm grateful that he's dropping the issue, even though he doesn't totally believe me. I really wasn't lying. I just didn't elaborate. There is a difference. Really.

Returning home, he picks Petunia up and gives her the love she acts like she doesn't want. They head back to his room to unwind and unpack leaving me gloriously alone. I lay down on the couch, and Freddie jumps up and takes his place on my stomach. He does his normal circle, three times counter clockwise and then plops down unceremoniously on my belly. He's asleep and snoring within seconds. Oh, to be a dog. That would be the life, right? Belly rubs whenever you want, someone to take care of you, to cuddle you, and love you.

You wouldn't have to work. I mean, even though he is a therapy dog, it doesn't seem like a strenuous job. At least with me it isn't. I wish I would've been a dog.

With that in mind, I realize I have completely lost all hope of being normal and shut my eyes for a nap. It's only about 9 pm, but I don't feel like going to bed yet, since I slept so late this morning. Listening to the music coming softly out of Quinn's room, I just breath. I wish the heaviness in my chest from the dream would go away. It's been coming and going all day. It makes me sadder than I normally feel, but this time it's for someone else.

In my life, I have only cared for my family, in the 'family love' kind of way and for Quinn. Again, like family. He's my twin brother in every way, but biologically, of course. He's the person I'm closest to, yet I don't ever recall feeling like this toward him. I mean, I've wanted to help him feel better and get over things, but never to the depth that I feel it in my chest now. Even with Quinn and my family, I keep my distance and a wall up. I feel uncomfortable energy, no matter who it is, when they're having a crisis.

As I try to ponder it all out, I receive a heavy smell of Zeke. With my eyes closed, I sense him sitting on the floor beside me. In my head I see him put his hand up and over my chest, right above my heart where the heaviness is located. I barely hear him, but more sense his words: "Let me take this pain away. It was never meant for you. This is mine and mine alone".

"No Zeke, I want to help you carry it. It connects us somehow. I don't know why and I don't understand it, but it's something I need to do for you." I drift off into a content sleep with his smell and warmth still surrounding me.

Lacie Minier

Chapter 12

Gertie

Over the next two weeks, I finish the book. After I had the experience of Zeke's death, and the conversation we had about me and how I feel in life, the words came easily. Everything flowed smoothly. I spent my days writing, only taking breaks to work on my other work. That gave my brain a well needed reprieve from my story, and more importantly, kept me in good standing with the editors I work for. I've drastically cut my hours since the accident, but I want to keep up my skills, and of course, keep up my employment, even if it's part time for now.

This morning I started editing my book. I'm not usually a vain or cocky person, but I feel this is a really powerful and moving book. I put a call into Bob, the one editor-in-chief that I do the most work for and who I get along with the best, to see if he'd be interested in reading the book for me. I'm anxious about his response and eager for his thoughts and ideas.

I've also been anxious because Zeke hasn't been around since the day after the last dream. I haven't noticed his smell or sensed his presence. I don't like how lonely I'm starting to feel, again. I've always felt lonely until I met him. Then suddenly, someone 'got me'. He understands me on a level that no one else ever has. That alone was making me feel less lonely.

I've never met someone who I immediately felt a connection with, someone who I could trust. It's like I knew him before, but I couldn't have. He lived states away and never crossed my path. We just have so many things in common that I guess that's the connection I sense. I think that is why I feel... I don't know, restless without him, maybe? I became so comfortable having someone who understands me and made me feel less alone, and now he seems to have disappeared.

My cell starts ringing beside me.

"Hey Bob, what's up?"

"Hey, Gertie! Holy shit, are you kidding me? You wrote a book? Of course, I want to read it. You are my most talented editor. You are also one of the most unique people I know. I can't wait to see what talent you have hidden in that head of yours. When can I get it?"

"Oh, good lord! I literally just started my re-read and editing of it this morning. Can you at least give me a week to make sure I have no glaringly embarrassing issues first? I kind of just sat down and wrote. I really need to make sure the flow is good and that nothing is completely missing. I don't trust myself to just hit send. Next Monday? How about if I send it to you then?"

"Oh, you tease. Ok. I give you a week, but I can't wait. Tell me what it's about, at least? Throw an old man a bone!"

"Bob, you're not that old. It's actually hard to explain, and that's also why I want you to read it. I need help picking a genre and writing a blurb. I really don't know much at all about that type of stuff. I would love to see if I can get it published, but I normally only pay attention to the editing and proofreading; I'm at a total loss for what else needs to happen. Help?"

"Of course, Gertie. Send it to me next week, and I'll give you a call then. I'll try not to get too excited and be patient. Try…but I promise nothing."

"Thanks Bob. Have a good one."

"You too Gertie."

Chapter 13

Gertie

"Oh my God! What is it with me coming home to that evil music blasting through our house? Turn that damn devil man off. I'm not subjecting Freddie to such crap!" Yelling at Quinn, I pick Freddie up and cover his ears while receiving a wet tongue facial in greeting.

"Oh stop. The Smiths aren't evil music and Morrissey isn't the devil."

"So you say. I tend to think his voice sounds like fingernails down a chalkboard. Seriously, you know the rule, no devil Smiths/Morrissey music in the shared public space; turn it off, or I'll break whatever speaker it's coming from."

"Oh, for Pete's sake. Ok." Picking up the remote, Quinn turns on the radio instead. This time Led Zeppelin comes through.

"Oh, this is music. So much better! Thank you, my love."

"Girl, you need to branch out with your music choices."

"Dude, just because I don't like your weird emo music doesn't mean I'm stuck in a music genre. I love lots of things, 70's classic rock and 80's hair bands just happen to be my favorite." I state confidentially.

"And what about your love of all things Peter Cetera and Bryan Adams? You're a ballad loving Queen. A diehard romantic at heart. Don't even try to deny it."

"I proudly acknowledge them as favorites, and my choices to sing to in the shower. Nothing like a good ballad to move the feelings in your heart."

Quinn laughs loudly at me. "You mean your dark, cold heart that you don't let out to play with others?"

"That's the one. It's saved for Peter and Bryan. Now, what are you cooking? I'm hungry and ready to celebrate!"

"What are we celebrating?"

Smiling larger than I probably ever have, I announce, "I've finished my book. I edited what I could, and I had one of my fellow comrade editors in arms help me. Then I sent a copy to Bob. He loved it! He's sending it to the big wigs to see if he can get me published." I'm practically jumping out of my skin. I've never felt this excited about anything before. Zeke and I did it! I wouldn't be here or have this chance without him, and I'm so excited to share this with him. I just wish he was here, too.

"Oh, Christ on a cracker! Are you serious? That's excellent!" Running over to me, Quinn pulls me into a bear hug.

"I'm serious and I can't breathe. I love you and all, but don't kill me yet."

Laughing, he loosens his hold. "I'm so proud of you, first off for finishing it, but more importantly, for accomplishing your lifelong dream and meeting a challenge you set for yourself. In so many ways I'm proud of you for that, Gertie. You overcame a big obstacle there, but then to have the confidence to send it to a co-worker of sorts, and let others read your work? And to send it to Bob? That's so beyond awesome and outside your norm. This is almost overwhelming!"

Shaking my head, tears start to roll down my cheeks. "I know. And thank you for caring and being proud of me. You always were the only one that knew me. My parents don't understand me so I'm fucking lucky to have you, Quinn."

"Ok, I almost want to be worried. You're never sappy and honest like that. Are you sure you're Gertie?" He chuckles. I know he's deflecting the seriousness, but I'm okay with that. He and I aren't known to be sappy or overly deep with each other. Sarcasm is our show of mutual love, respect and devotion. Geez, Zeke's bringing the stupid and sappy out of me.

"Yep, and now it's over. Ok, what's for supper?"

"I'm making lasagna and salad. I just put it in the oven so it'll be about an hour till it's ready."

"An hour? I can't wait that long. I'm hangry"

"Ha. No, you're hungry and excited! I'm not even going to try to combine those two into a word. So we'll sit, and you'll tell me about the book. When do I get to read it? You've been very quiet about it."

I nod. "Yeah, I have. It's been a labor of love in a way. It's not a happy ever after kind of book, really. It's a story about a boy who grows up with parents who rule his life. They make him do everything they think he should; they don't care how he feels or what he wants to do. He's not allowed to make any of his own decisions. The book goes through different periods in his life and shows the internal struggles that war within him. The struggle to keep everyone in his family happy and peaceful, meanwhile he's in hell and hating himself. It takes you on an emotional rollercoaster ride. In the end, the man kills himself to try to finally find peace. It's the first real decision he gets to make on his own, and it ends up being his ultimate eff you to his parents."

Leaning back against the counter, Quinn tilts his head at me. "Suicide. Didn't expect that from you. You've never contemplated it yourself, have you?"

"No. I'm too lazy to do that. But I heard a story about a guy like this, and it stuck with me. I felt the need to tell it, so hopefully, other people will see just one of the reasons why people do try to find peace in suicide. I'm thinking of a follow up book explaining his struggles on the other side of suicide. His quest to find peace and show how it may or may not happen."

Quinn nods. "Those both sound really interesting, surprisingly. I'd love to read it sometime, if you'll allow me to. Did you use any of the brainstorming ideas we came up with on our drunken night?"

"Actually, yes, I used the names of the characters. Didn't I tell you the premise of the book then?"

"Hell, you might've, but we were plastered. I'm surprised anything that came out of that night was useful."

"Truth, dude. Complete and utter truth."

As Quinn grabs glasses of ice tea I head to the living room. I know I need to tell him about Zeke. I really do. I don't want to keep Zeke a secret, but I don't know how to go about it, yet. I want to be able to talk to Quinn about Zeke's struggles. I want him to know how Zeke's helped me, but also how he's brought up all these damned thoughts and given me weird feelings. Quinn is the only person who can help me sort out how I get when I'm around Zeke or thinking about him. Yet, I can't seem to do it.

Quinn's going on and on about his current client and how much of an ass the old guy is, but he pays well, so he's dealing with the guy. I notice myself zoning out and thinking about Zeke more and more. It's been weeks since I got to visit him, and it scares me that I miss him. It also scares me that I can't seem to visit him as I did before. I'm afraid that since the book is done, they've moved him on, and I won't have him as a part of my life anymore. These last couple months have been the best ones I've ever had.

It's not just accomplishing my writing dream, or how I'm loving the experience thus far, but it was the openness with Zeke and being with him. The calmness I felt in his presence. The getting to know him, and the talks and laughs we had together. The feeling of finally being complete. I never had that with anyone. Pathetic, huh? I can't seem to find this connection with anyone living; no, I have to connect with a dead guy. This is true Gertie form at its finest.

The buzzer on the stove goes off, and Quinn finishes getting everything ready as I go to use the bathroom. Splashing water on my face to bring me back to the present, I try to ground myself and take deep breaths. Boy, my mood shifted drastically. I was so excited and then crashed. I want Zeke here to celebrate with us. Without him, it just feels, well, incomplete. I so don't know what to do with these emotions. This is all so new, and now, I can't even talk to him about it.

Looking at myself in the mirror, I see nothing has changed, yet, I feel different. I'm not sure I like this feeling. I don't like change. I really don't like the thought that I need someone else to feel complete, especially when it's a dead guy. I mean, can they be relied on to be predictable and around when you need them? I can't live my life *with* him and include him in things, not really. I can't even touch him for fucks sake!

Pasting a fake smile on my face, I head out for supper. Maybe some food will help me pretend I'm still excited.

Lacie Minier

Chapter 14

Zeke

Surprised at the presence of someone else, I look up and see Gertie. I haven't been allowed to visit her since our book is completed. Not sure why, but my visits have been cut off completely. I don't like it. I miss her.

"Hey babe. What you doing here?"

"I just got off the phone with Bob, my editor boss. I have to go to Michigan to pitch my book. They're making me do it in person. Damn it! I was supposed to be able to just do it through Skype. I hate airports, I hate people, and I hate standing in front of people trying to convince them something I did is any good. I mean, what the hell? He knows I'm awkward! This is like the kiss of death for the book."

Bingo. I don't know exactly how I do these things, but I made it happen. She's clearly not happy, but tough. She has a job to do. For me this time.

"Michigan, huh? Any chance you're going to be near Ann Arbor?"

"Yeah, actually. That's where they're sending me. Why?"

"That's where I lived and went to college. Roman's still there in our old apartment." I say nonchalantly and let the words linger for a minute.

"Huh, he still lives in your old apartment? Where you died?" She questions as she scrunches her nose and cheeks up. By God, this girl is adorable.

I laugh, "Yeah, you think that's a little creepy, too? I guess being a doctor he deals with death a lot so it wasn't a big deal for him."

"I call bullshit. He lived with you for how many years? It would've been a huge deal for him. Why wouldn't he leave? That seems really odd."

"I think so, too. No matter how many times I visit him, I can't figure it out. There's something there that I'm missing, and I think it's another reason I can't completely move on."

Not a total lie. I may have only visited him once, but I still haven't figured it out. A little push here and there should work with her. I've learned a lot about Gertie over the months, and if it seems like it's her idea, then she's better with doing it.

"Huh." She says while staring out in front of her. I can see the wheels spinning in her head.

We sit quietly for a little while and finally she says, "You need me to go see him, don't you? You just don't want to ask."

I can't help but laugh. "You know me too well, Gert. Yes, I do want you to go see him. You pick up emotions that I can't, and people open up to you without a second thought. It's your empathetic gift. They sense it somehow and feel comfortable with you. Which, that's really strange since you hate people. Usually you give off a 'stay away' vibe, but yet, I've seen it happen to you more than once where someone gravitates towards you. This would be a great opportunity for you to get to know me better through Roman, and I think it'll help Roman somehow, too. Plus, maybe I can get some answers to the questions I still don't know to ask."

Looking over at her, I'm knocked down by her big, beautiful blue eyes. My God, I can openly see her soul in those things. They shine so bright when she's with me and are so dull when she isn't. I hate seeing them dull and lifeless. When I look deep into them, they make me feel like she's looking right through me and into the depths of my soul, which she probably is. That used to scare me when we were first met, but now I love it. She fills that connection I was missing with others. It's like she is a lifeline for me.

Looking out at the waterfall, she nods. "Ok. For you, I'll do it. Is there anything you specifically need me to ask him?"

I shake my head. "No. Just talk to him. Let him talk about whatever he needs. If I get any other insights, I'll let you know, but I feel like he needs you."

She nods again. "Ok. Again, remember, this is for you. This whole trip is going to be a big thing for me to do. I need you to understand that. I wouldn't purposefully go to someone I don't knows house under any conditions, normally. It's just stupid. See, I knew you were making me stupid."

How is it she always makes me laugh? "Ok, blame me for your stupidity. I'm good with that. I really appreciate this, Gertie. You don't know how much you've already helped me."

Turning to me, she smiles. My breath leaves my lungs, and I feel like I can't breathe at all now. This is a full-on smile, one I've never seen from her before. She looks slightly shy, yet so happy. She's so different and so beautiful like this. Her whole face lights up and transforms. I really wish she could see herself through my eyes.

"Yeah, back at you. I'd never have sat down and wrote a book without your support and your story. I've never felt a strong enough connection with a story to actually do it. Yours, well yours needed to be told. The book is all you Zeke. My personality and sense of humor may come out scattered throughout it, but in very few places. In all seriousness, which is very unlike me, your story will help others, and I'm honored to be the one to tell it."

Seeing the brutal honesty and vulnerability in her eyes, I direly need to hug her, but I can't. Trying to put my hand on her arm, it again falls through her. "Dang it. I so need to hug you right now, Gertie. This is killing me."

Smiling sadly, she looks down to where my hand landed. "Yeah, I totally get that."

While we're sitting quietly, I contemplate the real reason we were placed together. Every time we're allowed to be side by side feels like so much more than just that moment. There is a strong connection forming between us. Butwhy?

"Ok Zeke, I'll go pitch my book and see Roman. Just, please, be with me for my flights so I stay relaxed. Not sure there is enough Xanax in the world to do it otherwise."

I smile. "You got it, girl."

Lacie Minier

Chapter 15

Gertie

Stepping up to the door, I pause. Am I really going to do this? Just knock and approach a guy I've never met to try to get more information about, and for, Zeke? If he didn't need me to do this for him, and possibly for Roman, I'd so not be here. It's weird I need to know more about him, that I have such a strong pull to help him, especially since it's completely out of my comfort zone. I don't understand any of this, but from the moment my boss told me I had to come here to pitch my book, this was all I could think about, meeting Roman. Then when Zeke hinted at it, I knew this was my main reason for this trip.

I stare at the door. Ok, put on your big girl panties and knock. Zeke knows you're here. He's with you and won't let anything happen. Why stall? Uh, social anxiety much? Duh. Ok, I can do this. Quickly raising my hand, I finally knock. Hearing movement inside makes me instantly feel like I'm going to throw up. Heart racing and palms sweating.

"Uh, coming?" I hear through the door. Great, he's just as confused as I am. Perfect start.

The door slowly opens and instantly, I smell Zeke and feel myself relax a little bit. Damn, that man... wait can I call him a man? I still don't understand that, but that soul knows me well. A very tall, very tan and very well-built man answers the door in scrubs. "Uh, hello?"

"Are you asking me hello or telling me?" I can't control my snarkiness since I'm nervous. I'm such a loser.

Smiling down at me, he puts his forearm against the door and leans. "I think I'm telling you. I'm Roman. What can I do for you?"

"Uh, well, this is strange I know, but my name's Gertie and I just wanted to meet you and ask you about your old roommate, Zeke. Is this too strange? It feels strange." Someone needs to help me and stop me from babbling.

He looks confused and sad. "Yeah, a little bit, but sure. Come on in. You look harmless enough."

He moves out of the way and allows me into the apartment. I walk into a huge open space with a kitchen and living room that flow together. Just how I saw it in my dream. The room hasn't changed, at all, in seven years.

"Uh, thanks for this. I give fair warning, I babble when I'm nervous, and I'm socially awkward so there'll probably be a bunch of babbling. Feel free to stop me at any point. But I really appreciate this."

Nodding, Roman looks like he's trying to stifle a laugh. "Not a problem. I admit, this is very strange. In all the time I knew Zeke, and since he's been gone, no one's ever asked about him or come to visit. All his 'so called friends' from college never even visited. So, how did you know Zeke? Did you go to college with us?"

I wasn't planning on lying to Roman, but he's given me a reasonable explanation. No, I can't do it. I can't lie. It's not me. "No, we'd met after college." Ok, that's good. Not a lie, but not the whole truth. I can deal with that.

"Oh, that's cool. I know that I was the closest person to Zeke, he told me that many times, but I have to tell you that I barely knew him. He wasn't the type to open up and talk much about himself. I knew him from freshman year all the way till he died. So what, like fourteen years? But I never actually really *knew* him. I guess he could've said the same about me. We knew all the unimportant things, surface stuff, like what foods to buy for the other at the grocery store or what to pick up at the drive thru. We knew what the other drank. Those kinds of things."

"I can see that. He seemed like the strong, silent type."

Roman smiled. "That's a good way to describe him. He was like an anchor for me though, through school and my internships. He kept the room and apartment clean and me fed. I don't know what I'd have done without him. I feel lousy that I never did anything back for him. He was such a nice guy. Never asked for anything. Never complained. He'd just give that sad smile and quietly go about his life."

"Sad smile?"

"Yeah. Like I always felt that deep down he was putting on an act of some sort. He'd smile and laugh, but it never made it to his eyes. He had dull, sad eyes. I'm a freaking doctor. I should've noticed something was wrong, but I was too self-involved and too busy. I'd finally gotten residency at the hospital with decent hours. I could finally have a life and do things for him, and that's when he died. Just at the time I should've started giving back to him, he was gone." Roman's chin hit his chest as he looked down in his lap.

I don't know what makes me do it, but I lay my hand on Roman's arm. I don't know what's going on with me, but I really want to hug him. I can feel the guilt and sadness in his heart, and I want to relieve that for him, and for Zeke. I think a lot of what is holding Zeke back is how Roman's feeling.

"Roman, you have to know that Zeke wasn't the type of guy to believe you owed him anything. From what I know of him, being a giver was the type of person he was. Helping everyone else out and never thinking about himself. To be honest, I don't think Zeke ever knew who he was."

Roman nodded. "Yeah, I agree with you there."

"So, you said that no one ever came to visit him. No one? No family or friends?"

"Nope. His Dad would 'beckon' him home when they wanted to see him. I knew nothing about his family. I knew he had sisters, but had no clue how many or their names till the funeral. He barely talked about any of them, except maybe when they'd call, or he'd come back from visiting them. He was always off for a couple days when he'd get back. He'd be extra quiet and would stay in his room. I'd love to know the story there. Something wasn't right with that at all."

I totally get that. I really like Roman. Even though he's full of guilt right now, he's got positive energy. He saw more than Zeke knew. I wish Roman would've talked to him about it more. "So, no friends either? No girlfriends or anything?"

Roman smiled sadly again. "Nope. I don't even know if he was interested in girls. Or hell, maybe even guys. He never dated. No one ever called here for him. No one came over. He never went out. He would go to work and then come home. Sometimes he'd stop at a store or the bank and that was it. Literally, it. Every now and then when we'd watch movies, I'd make a comment about how someone looked to try to feel him out, and he'd just cock his head to the side and look at the person and shrug. I mean, it took me till college to figure out I'm gay, but I don't know if he ever knew who he liked, or if he liked anything at all. I mean, can a person be completely asexual?"

"Hey, you're the doctor, you tell me."

He laughed, "Well yes, they can be asexual, meaning they don't feel physical attraction at all. But mentally he didn't seem to care either. He seemed totally disconnected from other people. Does that make any sense?"

"Yeah. It does. Ironically, my roommate's the same way. We've known each other all our lives. Literally, we were born in the same room at basically the same time. Our mothers became friends, and we were brought up together. We've always been friends. He's like my twin, but that's exactly how he says he feels. No sexual attraction to anyone. He claims he finds neither gender attractive. I love him, but I can't help but feel that Quinn's just masking being gay, because of the way he was brought up. But that's a whole other story. Sorry. Did Zeke know you're gay?" I already know the answer to this, but wanted to hear Roman's thoughts.

"Not that I know of. We never talked about it, and I never brought guys here. In college, I had a male 'study buddy' in pre-med with me who was also my fuck buddy. He'd call or email me that his roommate was gone for a while, and I would 'go to the library to research'. I don't think Zeke ever knew. Once we got this apartment, I never had time to date. I'd hook up with guys at the hospital, since there were quite a few of us, that were working the long hours together and gay and frustrated. Zeke never asked and I never offered the info. Like I said, neither of us talked much about our private lives. He knew nothing about my childhood, and I knew nothing about his. How horrible is that?"

Looking over at Roman, I see sadness fill his eyes. I'm glad I came. Roman needed to talk about this to someone and had no one to help him grieve. "No Roman, it's not horrible. It is what it was. I know Zeke enough to know if you would've tried to talk to him about any of this, you wouldn't have gotten anywhere. He wasn't a talker. He was a guy who kept everything inside and to himself."

Nodding, Roman sighs. "Yeah, I guess you're right. It's always felt like I could've done more for him. Like I should've talked more. Tried to help take away that sadness he carried with him. I felt horrible when he died knowing that I did nothing to help him live."

We sat in silence for a couple minutes. "Roman, how'd he die?" Again, I know the answer, but I wanted to know what Roman thought.

"Well, that's the million-dollar question, isn't it? I came home from a hellish night at work to find my roommate on the couch. I thought he was just sleeping, so I started talking to him and telling him about the craziness of the night. I looked over and noticed he hadn't moved and his eyes were shut. So, I walk over and as soon as I touched his arm; I knew. He was cold and then I noticed the smell. That death smell. If you don't know what I mean, I won't elaborate, because it's horrible. Apparently, working in the ER where I smell it often had made me immune to it when I got home. It kind of just lives in your nose. Anyway, I called 911 and explained what I came home to, and told them I needed the coroner. They came, took the body, and planned to do an autopsy since he was so young, and there were no obvious signs of how he died. We checked for asphyxiation, amongst other things, and there was nothing. They called a couple days later to inform me that they ruled it natural causes and decided against the autopsy due to 'family history' of certain aliments. In other words, I believe his Dad paid the coroner to not investigate."

"Why? Why would a father do that? Wouldn't he want to know?"

"You would think. I wanted to know. Zeke never drank, and I know he didn't do drugs. The doctor in me would have noticed those signs, no matter how busy or selfish I was, but deep down, my gut tells me he did it himself to escape whatever haunted him. Whatever caused that look in his eyes...that's what killed him. God, I hate that I did nothing. All those years. Seriously, I should've done something instead of brushing it off. The man was my rock during my education and internships. I would've been a zombie in stinky ass dirty clothes, who didn't eat or bath, without him around to remind me. I owe my whole career to him, and yet, I was a horrible friend. If I even was one! I feel like I just took and took from him and never did anything." Roman roughly runs his fingers through his hair before placing his hands over his face. This poor man's tormenting himself about something he had no control over.

I rub his back for a couple minutes in silence until he pulls himself back together. "Roman, I'm so sorry you feel this way. The whole way here I doubted whether I should come. I wasn't sure what you would think of someone just showing up, but now, well now I'm glad I came. Have you ever been able to talk to anyone else about this?"

Roman shook his head. "No. I've never had anyone who'd understand. I did try to talk to a nurse at work about it a couple days after Zeke died; he kept asking me what was wrong. I knew he wouldn't understand. He tried though, and I gave up. No one who didn't know Zeke would understand. Zeke was so different from most people. He was such a good guy and had a good heart."

He still does, only I can't tell Roman that. "Do you think Zeke finally found peace, Roman? And if so, shouldn't you be happy about that? No, it isn't the best way, and it kind of sounds horrible now that I said it out loud, but think about it. If Zeke is finally at peace, then shouldn't you be happy for him?"

Roman stares off at the wall for a couple minutes, and I let the question linger between us. "Yeah. I guess so. He did deserve peace and happiness. I really hope he found it."

"Good, now stop beating yourself up over something that you and I both know you had no control over. Yes, maybe you could've tried to talk to him, but I think we both know he wouldn't have talked. He would've blown off your question or given BS stereotypical answers. You're a good man from what I can tell. You need to let the guilt go and move on. And I have to say, while this is a really nice apartment, you may want to move somewhere that isn't a daily reminder that your roommate died here. I mean, to me, it's kind of creepy." I scrunch up my nose and give him a look of yuck.

Looking over at me, he barks out a laugh, which thankfully, is what I was going for. "Yeah. I've been thinking about that myself. I've been contemplating a relocation in general. I have nothing and no one keeping me here in Ann Arbor. I could really go for a smaller town and a less hectic lifestyle. I've just been lazy at looking up new jobs in new areas."

"I get that. The town I live in is the one I grew up in. Talk about small towns. I really should relocate to somewhere that doesn't have everyone up in everyone else's business. I mean, I try my best to be a wallflower and just blend in, but it's hard. I do love my small town, though. Less people equal less anxiety attacks. This city's huge and overwhelming. Thankfully, the meeting I came into town for is tomorrow, and I head home the day after.

"And what's the meeting? Anything fun and exciting?" Wiggling his dark eyebrows at me, he flashes me a mischievous grin.

"Well kind of. I'm normally a freelance editor and proofreader. I do it from home in my jammies and don't normally have to deal with people, except through email. I came into town because I'm pitching a book I wrote to one of the main publishers I do work for. They wouldn't let me do the pitch over Skype, like I requested, so I had to fly out here and do it in person."

"Huh, that sounds interesting. Where do you live?"

"A town in central PA. It's called Raineyville. If we didn't have an extremely expensive private college in it, no one would've ever heard of it."

"What's it like in Pennsylvania? That's one area I considered for a relocation. My grandparents grew up there before moving here in the 70's. I remember they liked it and talked about it a lot."

"It's ok. Weather is unpredictable at best. I live pretty much three to four hours away from all huge cities: Philly, Baltimore, DC, NYC...further from Pittsburgh. It's a nice location. Not much culture where I am, but I do visit the cities sometimes, and their galleries for culture when I feel stifled. Otherwise, I like it. I like small town living best. Everything I need is within walking distance of our apartment, and we have a creek out back that I like to go down and sit by. Maybe you should come visit sometime. You could meet Quinn and my Freddie. Freddie's my emotional therapy dog that the company wouldn't let me bring along."

Looking over at me, Roman smiles. I think that's the most genuine smile I've seen from him, so far. "I'd like to visit you and see where you live. I know this may sound crazy, but can we keep in touch? Just knowing that you knew Zeke, and that I can talk to you about him has helped me."

"Of course. I would love that. You seem like a cool guy. Maybe I can help you find a new place and a new job!"

I can't believe how this turned out. I'm so happy now that I came to see him. If this book doesn't get published, I won't be disappointed. My gut's telling me that this meeting was the important one I needed to have in town. This is the one person that Zeke and I can help. This is what made the last couple months' worth everything.

Chapter 16

Gertie

After Roman and I exchange numbers and emails, I head back to the hotel. I take a nice long bath in the huge garden tub, order room service, and pass out for the night. I loved meeting Roman, but it took a lot of my energy to get to his apartment, get through the conversation, and get back in one piece. Social anxiety and being an empath in a large city really sucks the life out of a person.

The next morning brings an annoyingly loud, ringing alarm. Stumbling out of bed, I immediately call for coffee and food. Room service is the best thing ever invented. Seriously. I don't have to get dressed. I don't have to leave the room, and I don't have to deal with people until the caffeine is pumping through my veins. See, the best thing ever.

After a shower, food, and my lifesaving coffee, I order up an Uber and wait in the lobby for it. Feeling vaguely human at this point, the nerves of facing the group of people I have to pitch my book to are settling in. Maybe food wasn't the best choice this morning. I don't want it to make a reappearance.

Sitting in the big, oversized chair in the lobby, that provides a good view of the front, I wait. My leg's bouncing and I'm fidgeting. My lovely nervous habits that I can't stop are all present. I do them often, yes, but it doesn't mean I like them. So, I pull out my phone and start scanning social media and email. What did we do to kill time before smart phones? Did people carry books everywhere? I don't remember.

Anyway, I'm not paying attention to anything I'm scrolling past in my newsfeed, because well, I'm too nervous to pay attention. Honestly at this point, I just don't care what my 'friends' had for breakfast or whose kid did what. I can't even believe that I have 'friends' on social media since I have none in real life. Most are people I don't even know personally, we just know each other through work. There are the people I went to high school or college with, and a few are family. Oh! And the occasional other freelance editors. Man, I'm pathetic.

Noticing the Uber pulling up, I make my way out and slide into the car. It's a nice little compact car, it has to be a luxury name brand. The man acknowledges my existence with a head nod and pulls out into traffic. Staring out the window, I watch the sky scrapers pass by. Feeling my phone vibrate in my pocket, I pull it out to see a "good luck" text from Quinn. I love the guy, but he's the emoticon king...or queen. I'm still not sure on that one, but I'm leaning toward queen. I type out a quick, thanks, and notice the car's already stopping. Looking up at the driver, who looks slightly annoyed with me, I ask "Are we here already?"

"Yep."

Well...Okay, then.

Crawling out of the car, I take a deep breath and head toward the lion's den.

What feels like weeks later, but is only a couple hours, I walk into my hotel room in shock that they offered me a deal right then and there. I believe Bob had a lot more pull on this than my writing, but they claimed they loved it and we set everything up. I sit down on the end of the bed and try to feel something. I've wanted to write and publish a book of my own since I was young, and it's happening. Why am I not more excited? Am I in shock? I feel numb, yet again, when I know I should feel something. I hate this.

The rest of the day I spend in my jammies on the bed reading, or soaking in the tub. I wish I could take this tub home. I need to talk to Quinn about renovating the bathroom. We need a tub like this.

Pigging out on room service, I try to get my bearings. I feel, well hell, I have no clue how I feel. I feel like I feel nothing. Not feeling up to talking to anyone, I turn off my phone. I hate feeling numb. Nothing in my life has ever gone the way I wanted it to, so now that it has, I'm totally at a loss of what to do. Also, I never went after what I wanted. This time I did and I got it. This is a whole new experience for me. I don't know what or how to feel. Sad, isn't it?

Walking into the apartment later the next day, I find a note from Quinn. *Have a meeting out of town. Won't be back till late tonight.* I feel guilty that this makes me feel relieved. I don't feel like talking to anyone, yet. I'm happy, I think, but I'm missing something. Like I shouldn't be celebrating this because I don't deserve it, or it's going to fail. Yeah, that's it. I'm not used to things going right so I'm still waiting for the bottom to drop out. Apprehension. That's what I'm feeling. Woo Hoo! Look at me working through these minefields called emotions.

Also, I realize the person I want to talk to about all of this is not Quinn, but it's Zeke. Isn't that just a kick in the pants. Zeke hasn't been around at all since I finished the book, with the exception of the time we talked about Ann Arbor. I wonder if he had something to do with that trip? My gut says he pulled some strings to make that happen so I could meet Roman.

I still smell and sense him every now and then, but as before, I often wonder if it's all in my head. This makes me feel uneasy and uncomfortable. I don't like that I got used to him being around, and I especially don't like it now that he isn't. This is why I don't like having friends other than Quinn. I've never had anyone else that I could rely on to be here when I needed them. I've never had anyone I needed other than Quinn. I don't like this new situation at all. I don't like needing someone. It makes me uncomfortable and twitchy.

Dropping my luggage in my room, I'm greeted by a wiggling Freddie. To me, there's nothing better in the world than a dog who loves you. He greets me with so much unconditional love and enthusiasm every time I come home. Everything in the world could be fixed with doggie kisses. Picking him up, I snuggle him till he's done licking and loving me all up. I know my little guy's getting older, but damned if I don't love him more each day.

I'll unpack later, because, well, I just don't want to right now. I'm an adult. I can do that. Lying down on the bed with Freddie, I rub his little belly till he's snoring. Cuddling in close, I shut my eyes, too. I know it's only three in the afternoon, but I don't sleep well in beds that aren't my own, and all the stress of the last couple days has left me feeling exhausted. I have no work that needs to be done tonight, so my executive decision is I'm taking a nap.

"Gertie, why are you sleeping in the middle of the day instead of celebrating? One of your life dreams came true, and you're here with me instead? Explain please."

Looking around, I see Zeke and I are sitting in our spot on the bench. "Huh, I've missed this place. It feels like forever since I've been here. Ever since I got the book done, you haven't visited me."

"That's all nice to know, but you didn't answer my question. Actually, just to be clear, it's you who visits me, if you want to get technical."

I smirk at his cocky tone. "And of course, you must get technical. I've always thought you came to me. Honestly? I don't know why I'm here other than I was exhausted from the trip and laid down to take a nap. My energy was zapped out, and I didn't feel like celebrating." I shrug because it's all true. I don't know what else to say.

"Why not? Aren't you happy? You're accomplishing something you once told me was your dream. You did it incredibly well, and you got signed to publish on your first try. What's wrong? I thought you'd be ecstatic."

Shrugging, I look away. "I feel apprehensive. Nothing in my life has ever gone the way I wanted it to. Nothing good has ever happened to me. I guess I'm waiting for the other shoe to drop...or whatever that saying is."

Looking at me intently, Zeke sighs. "Can I ask a question, and have you promise not to get mad?"

"Well, that's an easy way to get me to be on guard, instantly. Ok, shackles are up, what?"

"Do you ever think positively about anything in life?"

"What do you mean?" I ask, defensively, of course.

"I mean, like you just said, you're feeling apprehensive instead of happy. After the accident, when you were in the coma, you didn't care whether you went back or not. I'm not saying you are a bad person, so get that out of your head right now, but have you ever been positive and looked forward to something good happening?"

"I never had anything good to look forward to before this, I guess."

Tapping his finger against his lips, Zeke pauses for a moment. "What about high school graduation?"

"Nope. I was headed to college to accumulate a ton of debt in loans to get an education, so I could get a job to pay said loans. I was not looking forward to living in a room with someone I didn't know for four years of my life, while dedicating myself to learning things that I more than likely was never going to use on a daily basis."

Conceding my point, Zeke nods. "Ok. What about college graduation?"

"Oh yeah, I was looking forward to starting my life already in a chunk of debt. Plus, then I had to pay my own bills, find a job to pay for those bills, and let's not forget the loans. I was looking forward to finding a place to live, and buying everything I needed, for said place. I couldn't wait for the glorious life of living off ramen noodles for years."

Looking absolutely horrified by my answer, Zeke's mouth drops open. "Do you even hear yourself and how horrible that all sounds?"

"What? I'm not being negative. I'm being realistic. There's a difference. These aren't exactly all bad things, but they're real and they're the things I had to be aware of to be able to take care of myself. I don't see them as things to be excited or happy about. Although, personally, I like ramen noodles. Add an extra bouillon cube to them and some shredded cheddar, and they're pretty damned good."

"Oh, my gawd, woman. Seriously?"

"What, you don't like cheese in your soup? Are you too good for ramen? We can't be friends if you are too good for ramen. That's a deal breaker right there."

Laughing incredibly loud at my response, Zeke shakes his head and looks upwards like he is asking for help, or maybe patience. "We aren't talking about your love of cheese, or soup, and you know it. I'll give you the whole realism thing. But still, weren't you looking forward to living on your own, or the possibility of living with Quinn?"

Pondering that for a second, I realize that back then, no, I really wasn't. "Not really. I mean, yeah, I was ready to get out of the dorms and my parent's house, to have a place I could call my own. I did want someplace private to do my introverted hibernation thing, without the hassle of the parents telling me I needed to be more social, but I don't think I was overly excited about it. I don't think I ever felt excited in my life. Emotions aren't something that come easy for me, Zeke. I'm numb, remember? I wall up things like emotions."

Zeke's quiet for a minute, or so, and then sighs long and loud. He seems to be frustrated with me and my lack of sentiment. Aren't we all? "Why? Why do you wall up your feelings and keep them out? Why don't you let yourself 'feel' anything Gert?"

Wasn't that the million-dollar question. I'd love to know the answer, too. Looking him straight in those gorgeous green eyes, so he knows I'm not lying to him, I give him the best answer I can.

"I don't know. I've done it all my life and I don't know why. It's an instinct for me. I can assume it's from being able to feel others' energy and emotions, and it's overwhelming. Half the time, when I do open myself up, I can't tell if the feelings are mine or someone else's. So, that means I can't process them. As a kid, it must've driven me nuts. I don't remember. I appeared to have blocked a lot of my childhood out, or I didn't have anything worth remembering. I don't know which one, but I've thought about this a lot, and I honestly don't know. I wish I did. I wish I knew how to overcome it, because I feel like a walking zombie. Or a robot. Numb. When I'm out in public that feeling is great. It helps me survive. I don't know how to let it go or turn it off."

Getting antsy, I start fidgeting again. Great, even in dreams I can't stop my nervous habits. I feel so frustrated. "When I do open myself up, I've noticed that I only 'feel' negative feelings and emotions. I can feel nervous or frustrated, like now. I can feel confused, pain, sorrow, or hurt. Yet, I can't feel happy, joy, excitement, or love. Maybe a part of me is broken. I've been told by other empaths that my energy isn't negative, but how can it not be when those are the only things I can feel? Otherwise, I'm just like a robot walking the earth. The only positive feelings or emotions I've ever sensed were up here with you."

Saying all of this out loud is a first for me. Again, I'm telling Zeke my fears and thoughts with no hesitation. Things that no one else knows or has heard. I don't think anyone has ever taken the time to sit down and talk to me about this, except maybe Quinn. I feel myself getting very uncomfortable and defensive again, yet I can't stop it. Once it starts, it can't be stopped. I hate the feeling of not having control over myself.

"And why is it that I tell you all this stuff, when most of it, I've never even acknowledged to myself, let alone told anyone else? Is this some kind of voodoo magic you have up here that you're pulling on me?" Waving my arms all around, I continue to rant, I just can't stop myself. Feeling as if I'm going to crack in half has me out of sorts, and I have no clue why.

"No. You know it's not. Take a deep breath and hold it, Gertie. You're going into panic mode. Please don't do that with me. I'm safe. Keep breathing. To answer your question, it's that you need to let it out, and you know this is a safe space. You know it'll go no further than you and me because, well honestly, who the heck am I going to tell? You're the only person I'm assigned to, and only you can hear me. Plus, you know my fears. I opened up to you so you must feel like you can trust me on some level."

Blowing my hair out of my eyes, I calm down and sigh. "You know, I hate how logical you can be. It's annoying. Plus, you should know by now that I do trust you, more than is comfortable."

Zeke laughs at me, again. As awesome as his laugh sounds, it's not helping. Not right now when it is directed at me, and I'm still a little uncomfortable.

"Gertie, listen to me. We were paired together by something much more powerful than ourselves. It was for a reason. We've been over this. Just flow with it. Don't try to fight it; you won't win. Maybe we can get you out of 'zombie mode' and help you feel again. Not sure how, but hey, let's wing it. It's been working with everything else."

"Again, logical. I hate that."

Once again sitting in silence, I begin to relax. "So, what's your big plan here? How are we going to switch my mode to *living*?"

Tilting his head to the side, he bits his lower lip. "Not sure yet. Let me think about it."

Silently, I nod and look out over the water. Against my better judgement, there's something I have to ask, even though I know it's giving too much away. I know he's going to hear the hurt in my voice. "Zeke, why haven't we been able to have talks like this, lately? I mean, what happened that you don't come visit me? Did I do something wrong?"

Looking over at me with his intense, yet sad eyes, he shrugs. "I don't know. It's been bugging me as much as it's been you, Gertie. I wish I had an answer for you, but I don't. I wish I could make our time apart lessen, but I don't know how."

Taking a deep breath, I turn my head and stare back out at the waterfall.

Chapter 17

Gertie

Waking up, I feel something painful on my stomach. Opening my eyes, I find Freddie standing on my belly and licking my face. Picking him up, I get up off the bed. The clock reads 7:30 p.m. I take Freddie for a walk and come back and order Chinese; I'm feeling the overwhelming need for comfort food. Sitting down on the couch, I start flipping through my usual channels on the TV until I find a movie to watch, or at least for background noise. Picking up my phone, I find a missed text.

Roman: *Did you make it home ok? How'd your meeting go?*

This guy's such a sweetheart. He let me in his apartment and opened up to me without a second thought, and now he's checking up on me. I don't care why he's doing it; I'm going to enjoy it. Other than Quinn, no one ever texts me to check in.

Me: *Yep. Got home about 3 & took a long nap. Mtg went well. All systems go.*

The doorbell rings, and I retrieve my supper. Opening all the containers on the coffee table, I sit on the floor. Table to mouth level is perfect for lazy eating. My phone beeps again.

Roman: *That is so great! Do I get a free copy? I don't read often, but I need a new hobby.*

Me: *Sure. Want to be special & get it now or an actual copy when it comes out? And keep all your negative reviews to yourself. I only want to hear the positive.*

Roman: *☺ gotcha! Either. Both. Up to you.*

Me: *ok. I'll email it to you later when I get on the laptop.*

Setting the phone back in my lap, I dig into supper. Something about veggie lo mien makes my tummy a happy place to be. Ok, my tummy is happy, so apparently food is what makes me feel happy in life? Well, and coffee and chocolate. I wonder if there's a chemical in them all that makes me actually feel something? Do I feel something or is it a mental thought that I do? I know I should be feeling happy, so I tell myself I am? Holy shit, do I overthink everything like this?

Thoughts are jumping around in my head now like a squirrel on an energy drink. I can't seem to follow any of them, and I end up with a headache. I look down and notice that I finished off the lo mien and egg rolls. Picking up the soup and cold sesame noodles that I haven't yet touched, I take them to the frig. I clean up the coffee table and grab an ice tea. I'm restless and nothing catches my attention on TV. Looking at the clock I find it's only 9 pm. Without a book to write or edit, I don't know what to do with myself. Shower. I'll go take a shower and hope the water washes away all the strange ass thoughts jumping around in my head.

Zeke

Sitting on this darn bench staring at the waterfall is all I seem to do all day. While this is a beautiful and peaceful place, I feel no peace. I helped Gertie write her book and work through some of her issues. I helped guide her to Michigan and meet Roman. She helped Roman start to move on. I've gone back and I did open up some opportunities for my sisters to have a better life. So, why do I feel unsettled and restless? What have I missed that I need to do?

The more I think about it, the more frustrated I get. And the worst part is, I haven't been able to talk to Gertie. Again. I'd gotten used to laughing with her and having deep conversations. My time with her fed my soul and brought me peace. It's the only time I've felt that. I hate to admit it, but for once, I felt whole. She jokingly said that she thought if I was still alive we'd be the other's missing piece. She's right. Except I'm not alive, and she is. I'm now a being, a soul being held in a realm where I can't reach her. She's a soul still in human form on earth. So how's my missing piece a human, while I'm not? This is truly crappy. Is this my punishment for taking my own life?

Sensing that she's growing frustrated, I can't do anything about it. *They* say I've accomplished my duties and don't need further contact with her. I disagree. I'm connected to her, and I can feel everything she feels. Her numbness is falling by the wayside; I sense her uncomfortableness, fear, and frustration. I need to figure out a way to get back to her, but *they* have me trapped here. I can't leave this area. Every time I try to find a way out, I can't.

What do *they* want from me? If I accomplished my duties, then why can't I leave or move on? Why do I seem stalled? Running my hands up and over my face, I feel like this is what they told us Hell would be like. All I do is think, get frustrated, and nothing gets accomplished. I'm shown things going on below if I beg enough, but I can't do anything about them. It's torture. Why won't *they* let me make a difference? And who the heck are *"they"*? I never see anyone; I hear their voices. If I was still alive, I'd think I'm freaking insane. I swear *they're* trying to drive me crazy on purpose, but I don't understand why.

Standing up, I begin pacing, again. It never does any good, but sometimes I can calm down with the consistent cadence. Walking around the flowers, I turn to the waterfall, and ducking in underneath it, I stop and watch the water descend in front of me. The babel of the flowing water soothes me. I hide in here for a while, listening to the sounds of the water, before walking out. The whole concept of time here is something I can't get a hang of, either. There is no night, no darkness, so I can't keep track of it.

Strolling back to the bench, I glance up and there's another man waiting for me. I have no clue who he is. Just an average looking man sitting there watching me.

"Come here, Zeke. We must talk."

Ok. I wonder if this strange, and somewhat creepy, feeling is what Gertie felt when she found herself up here with me the first time. If so, I'm surprised she approached the bench at all. Walking over, I sit down.

"And you would be who, exactly? What do I owe the pleasure of your visit? I mean, I've been trapped here, wherever here is, for who knows how long without being able to DO anything, or help anyone again, so why come now?"

Ok, so apparently, I'm not good at hiding the frustration *they* are allowing me to feel, and my sarcasm is still sharp. Good to know.

The other man smiled. "Oh, you're a frustrated one, aren't you? Good! I like feisty ones. They're the most fun to work with and see the changes. I like that you're frustrated; it means you've worked through your issues enough to be allowed feelings again. My name is Gabriel. I've been sent to give you some answers. To help you understand."

"Well it's about frigging time. Oh heck. Why can't I swear? Please? It's my one true vice, and it frustrates me that I can't."

"Yep, that one took me forever to get used to, but once your soul finally settles and finds complete peace, you won't want to swear. Trust me. I was a lot like you once. I took my own life, also. And it took me much longer than it will you, to settle in and find the peace you're looking for. From what I've been told, I was the stubbornest soul that came through here. That's why I like the feisty ones. I resonate with them. I understand them. So, what do you want to know, first?"

Turning back towards the waterfall, I feel confused. "Dude, I have no clue. I have so many questions, and I don't even know where to start. I guess this one, why did it take so long for someone to come here and explain? I've been wandering around for years. What was the purpose of the time alone?"

"You were left on your own so you could figure out what you needed most. Whether you know it or not, you've found that you need peace and happiness; you need your missing half of your soul. Which, to be honest, is pretty much what everyone discovers. Probably because you never had that in your last couple of lives, it took you longer than some to figure out. Suicides are always placed in solitary, for a while, to get their heads back on straight. You came carrying the guilt of what you did, and you brought all your baggage with you to work through. It's a form of punishment for determining your own time of death."

Gabriel looks out at the waterfall. "At least you have a beautiful setting. I was alone in a windowless white room with nothing to sit on, only the floor. The brightness of the room about drove me mad. Anyway, once you started working through some things, *they* decided you needed a chore to help you find some of your own answers. *They* wanted to help you be able to move on. Thus, you were paired with Gertie. She needed the push to write a book, which helped her work through some of her issues, and by talking it helped bring you some clarity. You both helped Roman, which was an added bonus none of us saw coming, or planned. Kudos on that. You tried to help your sisters, which also helped you find more answers and relieve some guilt. You did a great job and went above and beyond. We're all very proud of you, Zeke."

"Then why am I still here and not allowed to do more? Gertie needs me, Gabe. Wait, can I call you that? I was never a formal name type of guy. Anyway, she's gone downhill. I feel it. You aren't letting me see what's going on, but I feel it in my chest. She's frustrated, and feels uncomfortable, and unsettled again. She's confused and hurt. Maybe that's why I feel this way? We're connected now, and I need to help her."

Gabriel nods his head. "Zeke, call me whatever you want. I want you to be comfortable with me. And yes, Gertie isn't doing well. You're right; you're both connected, and you always have been. You're experiencing her feelings and emotions, and she is feeling yours. So as you get yourself worked up, she's also getting worked up. You're mirroring each other. So quite honestly, I need you to calm down for her. When you start to feel frustrated, take deep breaths and try to combat it for her sake. It could all be starting with her. Right now, that's how you can help her. I can't allow you to be in contact with her again, yet. She has issues she needs to work through, and she has to accomplish them on her own."

"Why? Why can't I help her? Honestly, and I can't believe I'm going to say this, but I'll never feel peace and happiness till I know she's ok. I don't understand it, but it's something I know deep down. She's the only thing that's ever made me feel complete, Gabe. Complete. Whole. Peaceful. I need to be with her to help her. I know I'm dead, but this is freaking killing me all over again. Is this punishment, too, because it truly feels like it." Hating that I sound like I'm whining, I do it anyway.

Gabriel looks me over with a new intensity. "Zeke, when you were in human form, did you ever love anyone? Or feel love at all?"

"No." I answer quickly, and firmly. "No, I did not. Not even with my family. I kind of hated them for dictating my life. I never let myself open up to anyone, nor did I let anyone get close to me. Love wasn't something I was interested in."

Gabriel nods. "So that's why you don't recognize what you feel for Gertie. Zeke, it's always hard to know your love is hurting. You'll always feel the need to help her, but here's the thing that you don't want to hear, but you need to understand; sometimes there's absolutely nothing you can do to help them. They have to do it for themselves. It hurts us to watch them suffer, but it's something we have to do, in life and up here. There are just some things they must grasp for themselves to move on. She loves you, too, but she's never loved or felt real love, either."

Stopping for a second, Gabriel looks upwards then nods.

"Ok, full disclosure. You're ready to hear it, and *they*'ve granted me permission to tell you. Neither of you have felt love for hundreds and thousands of years. You've both been searching for each other for more lifetimes than even we can count. You were spilt up, very unfairly, very early in both of your soul's existences. You're literally the other half of each other's soul. You were made as one and need to be together to be complete. Neither of you have felt whole because of this spilt. You've both spent previous lives searching for the other since that horrible time. You always seem to miss each other."

Glancing over at me, Gabriel stops talking. I'm guessing he is gaging my reaction. I sit quietly and let him go on, eager to hear the rest of what he has to say. What he's said so far has made complete sense to me, even if it's odd. It feels right. These were the answers I've been seeking.

"The 'powers that be' have decided that enough is enough. *They* want you to be together once more and to be complete, happy. *They* can no longer handle watching your lost souls seeking each other. You both became complacent in this last life, and you gave up, which is unacceptable. Your decision to commit suicide eliminated any chance of finding each other. *They* don't want either of you suffering any longer. Since you both keep reincarnating, immediately, to go searching again, and yet, never find each other it was time to intervene. Pain and loneliness have caused you both to bring on your own death. For you, it was your last two lives, and for her it was the previous one to her current life. *They* deem it time to stop the cycle and allow you to be together again. You have learned all the lessons you needed to on earth for your soul's evolution, but Gertie has one more lesson, and it's one she must face by herself. Then you can finally be together again."

Nodding at him to show I understand, he continues. "This is why you were paired together after her accident. In all honesty, this is why the accident happened. So that you both could find ways to help each other, and to reconnect before she got here. You needed to work through your transition, and *they* believed it would bring her some peace. But it hasn't yet, not till she learns to open herself up to love again. She's fighting it and feeling unworthy. If she came here right now in death, her soul would need to go back at least once more till she fulfills this lesson. We've given her enough interaction with you for the love that is there deep down within her to bloom. She has to acknowledge it, see it for what it is, and accept the love within herself. She needs to open herself to the idea of receiving it, being worthy of it, and giving it to you. Then, and only then, can we reunite you two completely."

Looking out at the waterfall, I instantly feel relief. "So the end is insight for our souls to be together and complete? Because honestly, I'm exhausted. For as long as I can remember, I fought where I was and whatever I was doing because that integral piece I wanted was missing. I can't go on like this, especially now that we've been reconnected and spent time together. I hated to admit it before, but yes, I do love her. Deep down, I know I always have. It all seemed so odd and like it was too fast after only spending small amounts of time together. I couldn't understand how it was possible. As soon as you said it, I knew you were right. I hadn't felt it in so long I didn't realize what it was, but now I know, and it feels right. Strong. Passionate."

Gabriel nods. "Is there anything else you would like to ask?"

Leaning back on the bench, I stare out in front of me. I lace my hands together over my stomach. "There's one thing I'd like to do if *they*'ll let me. I want to visit Quinn, her roommate, and ask him to help her. She trusts him completely. Meaningful conversations with him should help her move through this lesson. I kind of understand why I can't visit her, but can I visit him?"

My belly drops when Gabriel looks down at his bare feet in the grass and shifts uncomfortably on the bench. "Not yet. Zeke, she's kept you a secret from Quinn. She hasn't told him about you, or your interaction. If you show up now, well, then he's not going to understand, and it could cause problems instead of help. If, and when, she tells him about you, then yes, *they* say you can do that. Until then, the answer is no. Help her by keeping calm on this side. She feels you, your energy, and your emotions as her own now. That was one of the benefits of your time together; there was a reconnection of your energies. She may not know it's your feelings, or emotions, or that you're connected, but you are and it affects her. You can help by remaining tranquil."

"Ok. But as soon as she tells him, can I go to him?"

Gabriel nods again. "Yes, then you may go."

Inhaling a deep breath, I hold it for a moment and sigh with relief. "Ok. Now that I know all of this, I can wait. I can be patient. I wish you would've told me this a while ago though. It would've been easier on me, which would've been easier on her!"

"Everything happens at the exact time it needs to, Zeke. Not a moment too soon or a moment too late. In life and up here. That's something you need to have faith in, my dear friend. *They* provide what you need, when you need it. In all your previous lives you both had opportunities to run into each other at pivotal points; these chances were provided for you both, each time, and one of you wouldn't take it. Free will, my friend. As bad as it sounds, free will has screwed over many people and souls. Ions of happiness has been lost because egos believe they know best and ignore gut instincts."

Laughing, I completely understand his point. "Yeah, I get that now, but that won't help me with the past. Oh, please tell me that I don't have to go back down there again, do I? Not going to lie, Gabe, I hated earth, and I can only assume I hated it every time and not just this last one. Why can't I remember the others?"

"You will. You haven't fully transitioned. You are in a limbo like state of being. We kept you here to wait for Gertie and to work out your last life. Once your soul fully transitions, it transcends, and you'll remember all your lives and experiences. Right now, you're still trapped, per se, in your last life experience. Does that make sense?"

"Yeah. Ok, Gabe. Thank you. I feel some relief now. Man, I was so frustrated. I hated not knowing and not understanding such important things."

Smiling at me, Gabriel nods. "For the rest of your time here, if you need any other answers, I'm at your call. Just say my name, and I'll come to you. OK?"

"Yeah. Thanks, Gabe."

Gabriel disappears, and I breathe out a sigh as relief washes over me. I wasn't completely crazy with my deep-down feelings for Gertie. It's nice to understand that when I feel complete with her by my side, there's a reason. I've been worried that I was so starved for a connection that I was creating it all in my mind.

Ok baby girl, I may not be able to help you the way I want to, but I'm going to overwhelm you with my emotions until you get it through your heart, and you have this lesson drilled into your soul. I'm tired of waiting for you. Let's get this done.

Lacie Minier

Chapter 18

Gertie

"Why did I let you drive? Seriously, you drive like an old woman. Do you know where the gas pedal is?"

"Quinn, shut the hell up. It's snowing for fucks sake. I'm not going to drive like a manic to get to my parent's for Christmas dinner. Which by the way, doesn't start for another four hours and they live ten minutes away. Chill the hell out! You're making me nervous."

"Oh please, the way you're driving we won't get there till 6:00, anyway. It's snow. We grew up here. It's not like you don't know how to drive in it."

"True, but this is a new car. I've never driven her in snow. I don't know how she handles in it. Plus, this road is curvy, and I'm not going to crash her. I love my new baby."

It's true. I really do love my new Juke. She's cute and has a bubble butt hatch like I love on cars. She's a shiny metallic blue and has a moon roof. I love her. Have I mentioned that, already? She has great new snow tires and traction control, but I don't care if she should be able to handle the snow. She's my new baby, and I hate snow. Freaking hate it beyond belief when I must drive in it. If I can stay home and watch it from my window, then it's the most beautiful thing. But not today.

"Oh, for the love of everything holy. Ok, I will shut up. I wouldn't want you to hit the speed limit of 35 or anything."

Oh also, did I mention that I love to annoy Quinn by driving slow? He can't stand it. He drives like he's in the Indy 500. Also, the reason I chose to drive today. I want to get there in one piece. He gave in when I rudely mentioned not wanting to spend another couple of weeks in the hospital. Yeah, it was low, but I don't care. I won the argument. Sometimes a girl has to do, what a girl has to do to get her own way.

As I slow to take the ninety-degree turn we're approaching, Quinn's mumbling under his breath. Something about me driving him insane. Is it wrong that I am really enjoying this? It is, isn't it? Well, hell.

I turn the corner and about forty yards in front of us is a deer, right in the middle of the road. Just standing there. Slowing down, I hope he or she moves out of the way. This is a narrow road to begin with, but they only have the middle plowed since it's the holiday. Coming to a complete stop, I stare out the windshield at the deer who is standing there watching us. Staring at us. Um…. can you say freaky? Or maybe creepy is better?

Why do things like this happen to me?

"Uh, ok. What do I do to get it to move?" Knowing Quinn won't know, I ask anyway.

"To hell if I know. I swerve around them. Can't your car go around in the higher snow?"

"Probably, but I really don't want to try it and end up stuck. And swerve around it? Really dude? Is that what you call what you do Quinn? I thought you just hit them to acquire new cars."

"Oh shut it, you bitch. I don't try to hit them. They jump out in front of me. I can't help that we have kamikaze wildlife around here! And most of what I hit are groundhogs or squirrels, not deer."

"I believe there should be some raccoons, chipmunks, and bunnies in that list, Quinn."

Flashing my lights at the deer, I hope it will scare it away. It doesn't. It remains standing there, staring right through me.

"Ok, deer. I love animals, and wildlife, and everything nature related, really I do, so I mean no disrespect by this, but there's a big old pot of mashed potatoes and gravy waiting for me at the other end of this road. It's a holiday for us humans. Could you kindly, please, step off to the side of the road so I can pass and go eat my weight in those taters? Plus, you're beautiful, and I really wouldn't want you to get hit by someone who doesn't care about you as much as I do."

I have no clue what possesses me to talk to the deer. I've always done this though, talked to animals, or flowers, or trees. A couple years ago I had a full-fledged conversation with a garden gnome in our neighbor's yard. Danny, our neighbor, caught me talking to George, that's what I named the gnome, and I was afraid to go back. I'm odd. Always have been. Have I mentioned that, yet? I like to think they understand me even though I know they can't. I mean they can't, right?

The deer was now about twelve feet in front of my car, but I'll be damned if I don't think he heard me. He cocked his head to the side while I was talking and stared right at me. As I finish speaking, he turns his head around to look at the end of the road and then looks back at me. Nodding, he prances off the road and into the forest.

"What the hell just happened? Did that deer understand you? Can you talk to animals, too? Why didn't you ever tell me?! You're freaking Dr. Doolittle, aren't you?"

"Quinn, I have no clue, but I have goosebumps. That was like twilight zone shit. I mean, there's no way he could've heard me, let alone understood me. I had good timing or something."

Slowly driving forward down the street, I shiver as I pull into my parent's driveway. Quinn's still looking at me strangely, and it makes me laugh. "Seriously, you actually believe that? That he understood me? You're crazy, you psycho."

Pointing a finger at me, he says, "You and your funky energy powers. I wouldn't put it past you to talk to animals. That... well, that was just weird." He punctuates his statement with a full body shiver.

I roll my eyes and walk up to the door, "Whatever."

Hours later, while sitting around the dining room table listening to my family babble on and on about whatever it is they are talking about, I'm enjoying the mashed potatoes and gravy just a little too much, oh, and the green bean casserole. Man, I love holiday food. My hips show the proof of that, by the way. I need to learn to cook this shit for myself.

As much as I'm in a love triangle with my taters, gravy, and string beans, I can't help but feel like something is missing, yet freaking again. I'm really getting sick and tired of this mood I slip into from this feeling. This unsettling and empty feeling resides in the pit of my stomach, and well honestly, I feel it in my heart, too. It's gotten a lot stronger, lately, and it's really starting to piss me off. It's more intense than ever. I'm restless, and annoyed, and I can't seem to put my finger on why, or even just knock myself out of this mood. I want to blame Zeke, but I'm not sure if he's the reason.

"Gertie, dear, how are your book sales going?"

Looking up at Mom, I smile. "Actually, very well. Apparently, Bob sent some free copies to some book reviewer friends of his, and they blew up the internet and newspapers with really good reviews. My sales took off over the last couple weeks. I got a check the other day from the publisher. I already sold more than I expected this book to sell in its entirety."

My parents beam with pride. I can't remember a time this particular look was ever aimed at me before. My sister, heck yeah. All the time. Me? Never. I get another unfamiliar twang in my gut. Could that be some sort of happiness? It feels kind of warm.

"That's so great, sweetie. I bought a couple and gave them as presents this year. Any of my friends who hadn't already bought one, got one from me, and now I can't wait to hear their opinions. I loved the book, although it's a bit sad."

"Well Mom, life isn't all rainbows and unicorns, is it? I just felt the need to write real life and all the shit it entails. It's what I felt needed to be said."

"I guess so, but books with happiness are so much better in this negative world. We need something good to escape into."

"I totally agree with you, Mom. I truly do."

Dad interrupts. "Hey, Gert, I thought you had another friend coming over today? What happened to him? We were looking forward to meeting a new male friend of yours." Winking at me, he wiggles his bushy eyebrows at me. I know exactly what he's thinking and will gladly burst that bubble right now.

"First Dad, Roman's gay so don't get any ideas like what's going through your mind right now. Second, his flight out of Michigan got cancelled due to snow and weather conditions. Third, because of flight cancellations, he decided to stay and pick up extra shifts at work so his co-workers that do have families could spend time with them during the holiday. He's an ER doctor and has no family anymore. So, that was why I invited him. He's a good guy. It makes me sad to think of him with no one. I don't want him to be alone."

Looking scandalized at the thought of anyone being alone on Christmas, Mom put her hand over her heart. "What happened to his family?"

"His parents were killed in some kind of accident when he was fifteen, and his grandparents raised him till he was eighteen. They were a lot older, so as soon as he went to college they moved, into a retirement community, but died soon after. He only really had his roommate, and then a few years ago, he died too. Roman's such a great guy. He's looking to relocate, and he's been checking this area out. Ironically, his grandparents grew up somewhere around here."

Mom looks horrified. "Oh, that poor boy. How'd you meet this man, again? I mean, if he's in Michigan and you're here…?"

"When I went to Ann Arbor for my book this past summer I met him. We started talking and became friends."

Dad shakes his head in complete disbelief, "Wait, you talked to a stranger? IN public? And became friends with him? I don't buy it. You don't talk to people, Gert. Especially not all willy nilly and you really, really don't talk to them if you don't already know them."

"Maybe he's really cute, and she was flirting before she found out he's gay, Dad. Don't judge. I have faith in my sister to act like a normal human sometimes."

"Uh. Thanks?" Giving her the stink eye, I'm trying to comprehend that she may actually have faith in me.

Shelly nods at me. "I'll stick up for you, lil sis."

Internally rolling my eyes, I shake my head. Like that would ever happen.

"We bumped into each other, and he seemed nice. Conversation started and flowed. He had nice energy so I went with it for once. I was nervous about the meeting so I started to babble, and he joined in. Don't question it. I ended up with a new friend."

Finally, coming to my rescue, Quinn offers his two cents. "He seems good for her. They text and talk on the phone. He makes her laugh. I don't know him, but I approve from everything I've witnessed so far."

I smile proudly. If Quinn accepts and likes him, so will the family. "Thanks, bro."

Now rolling his eyes, he laughs. "Yeah, whatever."

"So, he's all alone? It'd be nice if the poor boy could move here. We can adopt him in to our little family. Find him a nice boy to settle down with. A man with a background like that needs someone special in his life."

"Yeah Mom. I couldn't agree more. He deserves everything good in the world. I think he'd really like it around here. He saw the hospital here posted an ad for a supervisor resident doctor for the ER, or something like that, which is great, because he's more than qualified since that's what he does now. He applied last night when it popped up on his search. He probably won't hear anything till after the new year, but it'd be nice."

"Quinn, you deserve someone special, too. Maybe this Roman boy would be good for you?"

Holy shit! Mom has the perfect idea.

Choking on the drink he just threw back, Quinn turns to look at Mom with wide eyes. "Uh. No. I need no one. I'm completely happy as I am. But thank you, Lou, for the thought."

"Wheezy, leave the man alone. We go through this every time he's here. No wonder they don't come to visit more often. I mean, they're only at the other end of town, but are afraid to come here for getting hounded or hooked up with someone."

Oh yeah. Dad's full of truth there. Mom = 0, Dad = 1.

Mom's name is Louise. Most people call her Louie or Lou for short, but when Dad gets annoyed he calls her Wheezy to piss her off.

"Butch. Shut your mouth. I don't need a lecture. I can say what I want in my own house." Looking down the table at Dad, Mom tries to give him a stern look and fails miserably. Pointing at him, she adds, "You don't get any pie."

Quinn laughs at the threat, we all know she'll never follow through on it.

"Oh man, you guys should have seen what happened on the way here! Did you know that Gertie can talk to animals?"

"Oh, for the love of peanut butter and jelly. Don't start. It was a coincidence."

"I swear to your love of peanut butter and jelly that it's not. Ok, so, we were down here at the ninety-degree corner, and there was this huge deer standing right in the middle of the road. Gertie had to stop, and we stared at it while it stared at us. Very twilight zone-ish. Creepy as hell. Anyway, Gertie starts talking to it. I don't even remember what she said, but she asked it to move for its own safety, and her love of mashed taters or something, and it turned its head, like cocked it to the side, then looked all around and walked off the road. It freaking understood her! She has some freaking crazy ass powers, our Gertie." Quinn adds a cross of his fingers to ward off evil and pretends to shiver.

"You're kidding, right? You're not seriously believing this? I've known you my whole life, and this is the first time something I did worked perfectly, and you, all of a sudden, think I talk to animals. You're crazy."

Looking concerned, my parents look at each other then back at us. Mom looks uncomfortable. "Actually, Gertie, when you were younger you would talk to the squirrels and animals out in the back yard all the time, and they did the same thing. They would watch you, sit, and listen. It was strange. You eventually stopped when your Pap hollered at you for it. It was like he scared you or something. I don't blame you, that man was nasty. You were only, maybe four or five? Possibly six. You loved sitting out back there and waiting for your animal friends, as you called them. This doesn't surprise me. It's creepy, but it doesn't surprise me."

Sitting up straighter, Quinn pipes up, "Yeah, Freddie and Petunia cock their heads when you talk to them, too. I've often thought they understood exactly what you said. They always do what you ask. They ignore me."

"You're all crazy. I don't remember animal friends or talking to them. Can we have pie now?"

Dad shakes his head. "You never did feel comfortable talking about your gifts, Gertie. We know you feel other people's energy just like your grandma did. We know you can communicate with animals. You need to own that shit and not let it keep you down. Be proud of the gifts you've been granted. They don't bug us. We're proud of you no matter what, girl. Get out and live like your grandma. It's not something that should make you a hermit. Own your gifts. I worry about you sometimes being so anti-social."

"Dad, don't worry about me. I like my life. I have other issues that keep me inside and home. It's not being an empath and my empathness. Is that a word, or did I just make it up?"

Quinn laughs. "You're an author now, feel free to make up words."

Shooting him a look that screams 'well ok then', I grant him another eye-roll. "I mean, my social anxiety is because of chemical imbalances they can't seem to get regulated. I know it's because of the energy shifts I feel and sense; I've grown used to it, so I'm ok with it. Sure it sucks, but it is what it is. I've learned to deal with it. Please, don't worry, ok? I'm uncomfortable around big crowds for reasons other than my gifts. Plus, grandma was an extrovert to begin with, and she loved people. I'm an introvert who hates people. Big difference there."

126

"You sis, you hate people? Wouldn't have guessed that at all."

"Shelly. Shut your smartass pie hole and leave your sister alone."

"Yes, Daddy."

Mom gets up from the table. "Ok, before the shit hits the fan, let me grab dessert."

Lacie Minier

Chapter 19

Gertie

Hours later, Quinn and I are finally back home and settled on the couch in our fleece pj's, with hot cocoa and a big container of cookies that Mom sent with us. He scans TV channels before moving to Netflix trying to find something to watch. I text Roman to check in. He briefly responds that the ER is crazy tonight, and he'll call me tomorrow. Freddie and Petunia are curled up together in his dog bed and all seems right in the world, or at least it should. I can't shake the feeling that I'm missing something today. As far as spending time with the family, and holiday dinner with them, this year was actually kind of fun. No major arguments or problems. We were all pretty relaxed. Why am I feeling such discontent?

"So, what's been wrong? You aren't yourself, and I can't figure out why?"

Good question. "That's funny because I can't figure it out either. I have ideas, but no concrete reason."

"Gertie, come on. What's wrong?" Quinn looks at me with the most concern I've ever seen on his face. "You've been, well I guess off is the best word for it, for months now. Ever since the accident, really. Are you ever going to tell me why? Was there brain damage you didn't tell me about?"

Taking a long deep breath, I sigh. "No brain damage. Quinn, would you promise to hear me out completely, and not judge me if I tell you something you may not believe? Listen with open ears, open heart, and a shut mouth?"

Looking at me curiously, he nods. "Yes. Of course, I can do that. What's up?"

Glancing at Freddie, he instantly wakes up and comes over to me. Jumping up, he curls up on my lap, staring up at me with those big brown eyes, lending me love and support. He always knows when I need him. Even in the deepest of sleeps, he pops right awake and comes to me.

Petting him always makes me feel calmer. "Ok, so when I was in the coma, I kind of went…somewhere…there was this soul who talked to me. He was a lost soul and not exactly sure why he was there, either. He only knew that we had to help each other. We talked quite a bit before I came back, and then for months afterwards I would have dreams of just sitting and talking to him, or even meditating and talking with him. He told me about his past, and I told him about my dream of writing a book. I used his life story to write my book."

Stopping to figure out how much to tell Quinn, I take a deep breath and go all in. I'm surprised it took me this long to tell him, but to be fair, he's been away a lot for work, and I've been busy, too. Another part of me has been afraid to say any of this out loud because it's strange. People already think I'm a nut-job, why give them more to use against me?

Quinn looks deep in thought, while also, slightly confused. "Ok. Actually, I've read a lot of articles and stories like that. That's not unbelievable at all. So, what has you feeling off now? Do you feel guilty for using his story? Was he a real person at one time, or was he always a lost soul?"

"His name was Zeke Bradley. When he told me the first part of his story, he asked me to look him up, and I did. I found a lot of stuff on him, too, because he was a huge high school and college athlete. He was thirty-two when he died. He killed himself."

Quinn nods his head in understanding. "Like in the book. Wow. I thought you just made your character up from a vague story you overheard."

"Nope. He was real. His roommate, from freshman year in college until the day he died, was Roman. When I was in Michigan pitching my book, I went to visit him. He thinks I just knew Zeke before he died. He doesn't know what I'm telling you; I'm afraid to tell him. He's a doctor so I have no clue if he'll even listen to me, you know? When I was there, he told me a lot about his relationship with Zeke, and I think it helped him let go of the guilt he was carrying about Zeke's death. The poor guy believed that he could've stopped him, or that he at least, should've seen the signs."

Pausing a second, I reformulate my thoughts. "I don't think he ever really grieved before now. I believe that Zeke was sent to me to help Roman, if no one else, and to help me accomplish my dream with the book. He supported me and cheered me on the whole time. He let me run ideas past him and encouraged me to go with what I felt was right for the book, not what I thought others would want. He became my angel, even if he didn't like me saying it. He didn't believe he was good enough to be an angel. The dumbshit."

Quinn laughs. "Is that anyway to talk about your 'angel'?"

I smile. "I guess not. But I kind of got attached to him. Talking to him and being able to confide my thoughts of my past, or even my present was nice. Now since the book's been completed, he doesn't come around. I don't smell his scent anymore, either. That's bummed me out. I feel like he's missing from my life now."

Quinn's look sobered. "Why've you been talking to him and not me? I can't believe I'm going to ask this, but am I being replaced by a dead guy?"

"No. You're my twin, remember? Together forever as kindred siblings. He was there, and listened so earnestly, and asked me all the right questions. He shared so much with me that I started sharing with him, too. He helped me get over things I didn't even know I was holding in. It's hard to explain, really. The way we interact is different; I've never experienced it before."

"I don't understand, but I'll go with it for now. You're one of the most logical people I know, deep down under the sarcasm, so I don't doubt you. So, you're just sad that he isn't around anymore?"

"That's part of it...I have a general feeling of discontent. I've always felt like a piece was missing from my life. You know that. I've told you that often. But when we were working together on our book, we had such deep conversations, and I...shit I can't believe I'm going to say this, but I felt complete. I didn't experience that 'missing something' feeling once. But now it's back and feels stronger than ever. I don't understand it. And I sure as hell have no clue what to do to get over it. I don't like this at all." Hiding my face behind my hands, I try to breathe deep to calm the overwhelming sensation that is threatening to take over.

Looking at the TV, Quinn nods. Putting his arm around my shoulder, he pulls me into his side and kisses the top of my head. "I know that feeling well. Mine feels stronger lately, too, and it's pissing me off. I think that's why I've taken more jobs that require travel. I'm either trying to run from the feeling, or I'm trying to keep busy so I can ignore it. It isn't working though. Does this mean we're hitting our mid-life crisis? Should I go buy a flashy sports car?"

"Maybe! That may be the easy answer for us, but I have a feeling it's not the right one. I think it means we both really want a partner to fill the missing piece, that empty gaping hole that resides within us. And to be honest, as much as I hate to say this, I think that my missing piece is a dead guy. Just my luck, right? I can't even pick someone who's alive for fucks sake."

Quinn laughs so hard I'm afraid he's going to fall off the couch. "Yeah Gertie, I think I can say with confidence, only you would get yourself into that position. Honestly, I mean, how the hell do you get yourself out of that situation? Is there a possible win here for you somehow?"

"I've no fucking clue, Quinn. None at all."

Chapter 20

Zeke

"Zeke, I come with news."

Sitting up quickly from where I'm lying in the grass, I panic. "Is Gertie OK?"

Smiling, Gabriel nods. "She's fine Zeke. You would have felt it if she wasn't. Actually, how are you feeling right now? What do you sense?"

I'd been lying down zoning out, so I hadn't been paying attention. Shutting my eyes, I take a second to just feel. "I feel a sense of relief. A mild happiness, not much, but the start of it. Also, more frustration and some discontent maybe, but I feel….do I feel the start of love, something warm and encompassing? Is she finally realizing it? Admitting it?" I ask excitedly. My stomach is fluttering at the idea.

Gabriel nodded. "Sort of. She's starting to admit it to herself, and she acknowledges you as the missing piece. But, the thing I came to tell you is that you're now free to visit Quinn. She talked with him tonight, and she told him everything regarding your interactions and her feelings. She opened up to him; it seems she's starting to crack. I suggest you go to him soon. He's open to the idea of you, and he's the same as you in that he wants her to be happy."

Jumping up from where I'm sitting, "When, when can I go?"

"You're allowed to visit his room, and his room only, in their house. There are blocks, so don't try to leave it. You may go now and wait for him to sleep. Connect with him the same way you did with her. Fair warning, she may sense you so be prepared for emotional changes while you're talking with Quinn. Ok?"

Nodding my agreement, my body vibrates with excitement. I'm more than ready to get this show on the road.

Next thing I know, I'm sitting on Quinn's floor, in the corner. He's still out in the living room with her. I can hear them laughing over the TV. Just the sound of her laughter makes me smile and my stomach flutter. I want to go to her so bad, but I know I can't. If I try, *they* may not let me talk to Quinn. Or *they*'ll trap me again; I'm sure there's another name for me being stuck up there, but it feels like being trapped. Looking up at his bed, I notice a cat staring at me. Uh...ok. Can it see me? This may not be good.

She sits and stares right at me. It's kind of strange. This cat's looking at me like it knows I'm here and sees right into the depths of my soul. Sitting uncomfortably like this for hours, I finally hear movement out in the living room. It's probably only been an hour, but I'm impatient to talk to him.

"Alright Gertie, I'll see you tomorrow. We'll go for coffee. Night sleepyhead. And remember, things will get better." A man's voice says right outside the door. Must be Quinn. I feel like a weird stalker sitting here waiting for a man I don't know, in his bedroom. This is a first for me.

The door squeaks open and closes, silently. As the man starts to strip down, I look away. Ok, I'm now a creepy voyeur. Great. The things I do for this woman. I look at the wall to give him time to change. I feel like he's going to turn around and see me. It's unsettling. I still forget that I'm dead, and that he can't see me. The cat sure can though, and she's still staring at me. It's kind of freaking me out. I never did trust cats.

"Petunia, come here. It's time for bed."

Glancing back, thinking the coast is clear, I see him standing in boxers. Ok, that's better than naked. He's not a bad looking guy. On the tall side and incredibly thin with lighter brown hair. Does he have any muscle? His build reminds me of the guys Roman would watch. He never knew I saw him checking out men, and I never told him, but I knew. It didn't bother me at all, so why make an issue of it? I just wished he'd have found a guy to settle down with in his life. Roman's a great guy.

"Petunia, what're you staring at? Come here. You're freaking me out."

Oh great. Wonderful start Zeke.

Quinn comes around the bed and picks up the little furball. "Come on. Let's go to bed. I'm beat. It was a big day at the Meyer house, plus, I was subjected to Gertie's driving."

What's wrong with her driving? I have to know.

I continue to sit there while Quinn turns out the light and gets into bed. I have no concept of how much time went by when I feel the change in the room and know he's asleep. I can feel that Gertie's out too, and a general stillness settles into the house. It's finally time.

"What the hell? Where am I?"

"I'm so jealous that you can swear up here. I'm not sure how to explain where you are Quinn, but let me introduce myself. I'm Zeke. Please feel free to come over and sit down. We have some things to I'd like to talk to you about."

Tilting his head, Quinn studies me for a minute. He looks all around. After standing still for a minute, he shakes his head. "Ok, I apparently drank or ate something bad tonight, but what the hell." Slowly, he walks over and sits down on the bench.

I nod. "I understand the feeling. I had the same one when I first got here. I'd love to tell you the whole story, but I should make the most of our time. Gertie told you about me tonight, correct? You know the highlights?"

He nods. "Yes. I honestly never believed in the afterlife, or ghosts, or whatever, but I also never believed they weren't possible. Honestly, I just didn't care either way. But as she told me everything tonight I knew something like this had to exist. Gertie's not the type to make shit up, and there are way too many verified facts to not believe. If you really are Zeke, then I thank you for helping her with her book, but why disappear? You've hurt her by not coming back around."

Nodding slowly, I run my hands up over my face and take a deep breath. "Trust me, Quinn, that was NOT my decision. I've literally screamed and kicked things fighting to be able to go back to her, but *they* won't let me. And please don't ask who *they* are because I have no flipping clue. I'm being told she has a lesson to learn that she must work through on her own, and I can't help her with it. I have to leave her alone, and it's fudging killing me...well I'm already dead, but you catch my drift. Since she finally told you about me, I'm allowed to at least come to you for help. I wasn't allowed to contact you before this."

Quinn nods. "Ok, I can buy that. I see the truth in the pain written on your face. I don't have spidey senses like Gert does, but I can tell when I'm being lied to. You're not lying. I'm listening- go on. What can I do? She's my best friend in the world. I can't keep seeing her like this. What's the plan?"

Instantly, I like him. "Oh, thank everything holy. I was afraid you wouldn't believe me, in me or any of this. Ok. Not sure of an exact plan. You may have to come up with that on your own, but here's the story. The lesson she needs to learn is to open herself up to feeling love within her soul for someone else, and also to feel worthy of being loved in return. This isn't going to be easy, for reasons I can't tell you yet, but we have to find a way. She'll never find peace until she does. And quite honestly, I'll never have peace without her. Do you understand?"

Looking away, Quinn sighs heavily and nods. "Completely. I've thought this for years. She's so self-defeating, and she's always felt unworthy of everything, not just love. I can see in her eyes how much she loves you, but she won't admit it or accept the feeling completely, yet. I've no clue how to get her to realize that she deserves it."

"Me either, dude. I've been thinking about this since *they* finally explained it to me. And two guys aren't going to be good at this. I didn't understand the whole love thing either, not till I got here and met her. How am I supposed to figure this out and make suggestions?"

Quinn laughs. "I sure as shit have never felt love in my sorry ass life either. Not like that. I did from Gertie and Grams, but that's a whole different love then what you two feel for each other. I'm happy to hear you feel the same way,

136

though. I was worried, but I can see it in your eyes and hear it in your voice. But, uh dude, how can it work? You're dead and she's alive. Ok, I sound like a weirdo. Don't answer that because I really don't want to know. I'm on a mission now. I don't know how to do this yet, but I'll damned well get it done. I'll do anything for that girl."

Instantly, I feel bad for Quinn. "You've never been in love? Really?"

He frowns. "No. Honestly, dude, I don't even know who I'm truly attracted to. I've experimented with both genders and still haven't felt an attraction, let alone emotions, for anyone. I wrote myself off as a lost cause; I call myself asexual and go on with life."

Getting the feeling that's not the whole truth, I let it go. "Ok, we don't have much time, so here's the deal. I'm just a thought away. Don't freak out, but I'm only allowed in your bedroom in the apartment, but if you need me, go there and say my name. You won't be able to see me, but we can communicate if you sit, shut your eyes, and kind of meditate. Can you do that?"

Quinn nods. "Yeah I can. What about when I'm traveling?"

I think on that. "I'm being told that's free reign. *They* just don't want me anywhere near Gertie right now, that's why *they*'re limiting my access in the house. I freaking hate that so much."

Quinn laughs. "It makes sense, though. Hey, she mentioned a smell when she knew you were around. What's it of?"

Staring out to the water, I rack my brain trying to remember. "I think she once mentioned it's of coffee or mocha or something like that, but I'm not sure. Ask her. Oh! I see where you're going with this. Yes! Use it. Maybe if you inundate her with it, it'll help her?"

"Yeah, that's what I'm thinking. It can't hurt to try, right?"

Smiling, I nod. "Good thinking. Ok, I think our time's about up. Let me know if you need help. You can even ask for help before bed, and we can meet like this. Good luck, Quinn. No pressure, but I'm counting on you to help here, for her sake. Gertie needs you."

He smiles sadly. "No, Zeke. She needs you, but she'll just have to deal with me for now."

I nod and feel the flutter of my pulse in my belly. I really do hope she needs me as much as I need her, and I hope Quinn can get this done.

Chapter 21

Gertie

After carrying the last box in from the SUV, I look around the very small studio apartment. "Roman, are you sure this place is big enough for you?"

"Well, I pay per month with no contract, and it's temporary. So yeah, it'll be fine till I go house hunting. I didn't expect to be offered the job so quickly. I only applied for it three weeks ago and interviewed two weeks ago. I couldn't believe they offered it to me on the spot. I didn't have time to look for anything else. The hospital CEO offered me this place till I could get on my feet and settle into the area. Apparently, his son used to live here, but just ran off to backpack through Europe or something."

"Seriously?"

Glancing at me, Roman smirks. "No. But it's something that rich, spoiled kids do that people like you and I couldn't even imagine. So, basically the same."

Nodding, I chuckle at him. I'm happy he is here. "Did you hire movers to pack the rest of your stuff? How's it getting here?"

"Yeah. The moving company will pack the apartment up and relocate it here for me. I'll meet them at the storage place next week to open my unit, and then I'll go back and lock the doors when they're done. The hospital tacked on a nice signing bonus and moving incentive to start quickly, so I'm not actually paying for it. I'm just the middle man for the money."

Laughing at him as he waggles his eye brows at his own joke, I'm finding that Roman has a silly sense of humor, yet can be dry witted when he wants to be. His delivery of what he says ends up funnier than what he says most of the time. Half the time, I don't even think he's trying to be funny, and it makes me smile even more.

We finish emptying the boxes he brought himself, including his clothes. His huge SUV allowed him to at least bring all his essentials. The apartment is also furnished, so he didn't have to worry about that.

When I pop a pain reliever, Roman looks at me worried, with his eye brows all scrunched up.

"What? It's over the counter pain reliever. I'm not snorting crack."

"Why are you taking it? What's wrong? Did you pull a muscle or something?"

"No. I have a headache so I'm taking something for it. Are you going to go all doctor on me, Roman? It's a freaking generic Tylenol."

"I'll go all doctor on you whenever I feel the need to. You told me about the injuries from your accident, and I can be on edge if I want to be. But is it wrong to be concerned for a friend who just spent the afternoon helping me move and unpack boxes? I just want to be sure you're ok. Although, I'm going to ask, and you will answer me. How often do you get headaches?"

Rolling my eyes at him, I respond, "Roman, they're stress headaches. I used to get them as a kid but they went away around the time I went to college. They came back in the last couple months, but I know what stress is causing them so it's nothing to worry about. Seriously."

Roman's scrutiny makes me squirm. "Roman, please stop looking at me that way. It makes me uncomfortable. I really am ok. It's a slight pressure headache behind my left eye because I'm feeling sad lately, if you must know. Someone who came into my life and became important to me rather quickly, has done a disappearing act on me. I haven't seen or heard from them for about four months, or so, and I'm not happy about it. I feel lonely and slightly depressed. You know I hate talking about shit like this, but I'm only telling you so you'll back the fuck off the headaches. Ok?" I hate acting defensive, but he hit a nerve. I couldn't stop my reaction, or the tone of my voice.

Appraising me with a doctor's eye, he nods. "Ok. If you say you've had them before the accident, I'll lay off. BUT, and this is a big but, Gertie, I want you to have a CT scan done soon. After your accident last year, I want to make sure all is well in that head of yours. Ok? Promise me, Gertie. Please."

I can't say no to that. He's become too important to me. What's with all these guys digging into my heart and finding places in my life? It's making me become soft. I don't like it, but I do like having Roman in my life. I sigh heavily. Not comfortable with these changes in my life, I do what I always do and try to just push them out of my head.

"Fine, for you. I'll allow YOU to do the scan. I hate those machines and will need to be sedated, but I'll only do it if you're there with me. Deal?"

"Deal. I want to be there to see the results. I don't know any of the other doctors yet, so I don't have anyone else here I would trust you to. I may be an ER doctor, but since I'm the chief of the department, I can pull some rank. Once I get a schedule set-up, I'll make you an appointment in the next couple weeks, will that work?"

"Sounds good, doc. When do you start anyway? What are your hours going to be?"

Roman flops down on the couch, and I follow him. "I don't have a set schedule, yet. My first week's to get to know everyone and get used to the flow of their ER. I'll be seeing patients, of course, but there'll be other residents with me till I get used to how everything runs with their specific policies and procedures. I start on Sunday, so that's what? Two days away?"

Glancing at the display on his phone, he nods in agreement with two days. "God, I don't even know what day it is anymore. The last week's been a blur. Two days of packing and finding a moving company in Ann Arbor that I trusted enough to leave my stuff with, who could work on short notice, was fun enough. But then an almost five hundred mile trip that should have taken seven and a half hours turned into almost ten, with detours from accidents and road construction. Why I didn't pull off in Ohio and get a hotel room, sleep overnight, and then start back up this morning refreshed, I don't know. But I pushed to get here. Thanks for letting me crash with you last night till I got my keys. Your house, or apartment, or whatever you call it freaking rocks. It's beautiful and roomy, and has a nice feel to it. I really hope Quinn doesn't mind that I used his room."

"Nah. He told me to offer it to you since he'd be gone. It's more comfortable than the couch. After all the time you spent in the car, the couch would've sucked balls on your back. I'm glad that Petunia was on her best behavior and stayed in my room. She tries to get into Quinn's room when he's away; she pees on his bed, and in his shoes to punish him for leaving her with me."

"That cat's psycho. I don't think she liked me. The whole time I was there she kept looking at me like I was a murderer, or something. I think she hissed at me when I walked into Quinn's room. I'm surprised she didn't come after me and try to claw my eyes out."

"Don't take it personally, she doesn't really care for me, either. She only likes me because I feed her and clean out her poop when Quinn's gone. Sometimes I see her watching me, and I think she's plotting my death."

Chuckling at me, he turns his head to look at me. "Gertie, you freaking crack me up. You don't understand how grateful I am that I met you. I have no clue what or who in this big, wide universe to thank for you showing up at my door, but I need to thank every God, Goddess and deity known to man for that. You've changed my life so much. Thank you for helping me get this job and for listening to me. I don't know what I would've done without you."

Tearing up at his statement, I really want to explain that he needs to thank Zeke. I want to tell him about Zeke, but I'm afraid of how he'll react. I want to be able to talk to him about everything and get to know things about Zeke from Roman's prospective, but I can't. I just can't do it.

Batting my eyes at him, I try to eliminate the tears welling up in them. "Awe, shucks Roman. Thanks. Seriously, though I'm really glad I met you, too. I like having you around to talk to. You're a pretty cool dude. Hot too. Too bad you're gay."

Roman breaks out laughing. Early on I could tell that even though he initially opened up to me about Zeke, that wasn't who he was. He doesn't talk seriously about deep things or feelings, normally. We've connected by making each other laugh. Something both of us need more of in our daily lives.

"Too bad you're a chick. So...that's something I didn't ask before, how's this town about gay men? Are there many out and proud?"

"Uh... Let's see, how do I put this? You came to Pennsyl-tucky. There are more open- minded cows and goats than people. There's a church on what seems like every corner. BUT, that being said, no one's ever been harmed or threatened openly, either. I can't think of a gay person in town except a little guy that Quinn and I used to babysit. I don't even know if he's still around the area. I know they're here, but they seem to either blend in well, or they haven't come out to everyone. Or it's possible I'm such a hermit that I have no clue of my surroundings and the people in them. Maybe you should talk to Mom about this. She's a social butterfly around these parts; she hears everything, about everyone, down where she works. I'm sure she could set you up on a couple blind dates. She's constantly trying to set Quinn and me up with people."

"No, uh... thank you. Nothing against Momma Bear, but I like to find my own men. Honestly, it's too bad Quinn isn't gay. The picture of you guys in his room is kind of hot."

"It's funny you say that. I've always thought he's gay. He claims he's asexual, but I see the look in his eyes at certain people, all being men. He wants someone of his own. He's lonely, but he won't admit it. He thinks he isn't good enough for love because of his family background. Which, you know, really pisses me off since he's been hounding me for weeks that I need to change. He says I need to realize I'm lovable and deserve to be happy. Who's he to be all up in my face, to be like that, when he denies it just as much? Anyone who thinks my walls are high and thick should get inside his head for a while. I love the guy more than life, and he's like my twin, but damned if he isn't just as bad or worse than me."

Roman's quiet for a long time as I stew in this new-found anger at Quinn. It won't last long, it never does when directed at him, but why's he pushing so hard? Maybe I'll tell him as soon as he does what he's telling me to do, then I will too. We could make it a pact like almost everything else we've done in our lives.

Moving around in his seat, Roman looks at me with a crazy little smile, "I've been thinking it's time for a challenge. My life's been boring. When are you going to introduce me to the male version of Gertie, anyway?"

Oh boy. This could get very interesting.

Lacie Minier

Chapter 22

Zeke

"Zeke, seriously, I've got no clue what to do anymore. I've tried to be passive-aggressive so she doesn't pick up on all the suggestions I'm making. And I've tried leaving your scent throughout our house. I've suggested she writes in a journal to figure things out and to get her thoughts out; I believe that's what she's turning into her second book by the way. I've even been able to get her to talk to me a little bit, but nothing is breaking her down. What else can I do?"

Poor Quinn looks exhausted. I have to hand it to the guy, he's been working his butt off trying to get Gertie to realize that she's loveable and deserves happiness. I've been watching every step, and so far, I still feel her emptiness and frustration.

"I don't know Quinn. You've been doing such a great job. Even *they* think so. I guess we've got to let time take over. It'll play its course out somehow. Unfortunately, we have to sit back and watch. I mean, what're we going to do, brainwash her?"

"Ha! As if. She's too stubborn to let anyone do that. She's a hypnotherapist, remember? She may never use that certification, but she knows when someone's manipulating her. I wish *they*'d let you communicate with her again. She needs you. Not me. Not anyone else. You're who she needs and wants. At this point, seeing you may just help her give in. She aches for you, man. It makes no sense to me to keep you away."

"Me either, Quinn. I don't get it. *They* keep telling me that she has to learn this lesson by herself. But what's the harm? Maybe if I can't talk to her, but just sit with her? I can feel her frustration and pain. They are stemming from her believing that I abandoned her. That's what she's thinking, so how's she ever going to believe she's loveable if her 'angel' left her alone, and isn't there for her when she needs me? That makes no sense to me at all. *They* all say that this is how it has to be, but I disagree. I know her. I love her. This connection goes from my heart to hers, and I feel her pain. I know she loves me, too, I can feel it, throbbing in my empty chest cavity. It's there and strong. What do I do? Quinn, what do I do?"

I feel like I'm going to crack open and fly into pieces from the pain. Hers and mine. Why would *they* keep us apart? Deep down, I know Quinn's right. She needs to see me. She needs to feel my energy and know that I love her, too. She needs to know that I didn't abandon her.

We sit in silence for what seems like hours. Gabe's standing further under the waterfall watching us. I beckon him with my eyes and a slight head nod to join us, but he shakes his head no. Suddenly, Quinn jumps up. "I got an idea!"

"Ok, what is it?"

"Well, like I said earlier, she is a hypnotherapist and knows when she's being manipulated. BUT, she always goes to sleep with white noise running from her phone. What if, when she's asleep, I sneak in and set a couple of her hypnotherapy scripts to play throughout the night? If she's asleep, they should still work just as well, and hopefully, she won't consciously remember when she wakes up. She has ones for letting go of things weighing you down and loving yourself. That type of thing. I can look tomorrow. Do you think it could work?" Quinn's practically bubbling over with excitement at his idea. I can feel him vibrating.

"Quinn, at this point, I say try anything you can. Do it." I look up and directly at Gabriel to drill this home, "And I'll see if I can get permission to be with her in the hypnotic state. Maybe that'll help move this along. No talking! I'll just stand in the background so she can sense me and possibly see me."

Staring straight at me, Gabriel nods and disappears. I have no clue what that meant, but deep down I feel like he's taking my request to the 'powers that be' to see what can be done.

"Gabe, I was hoping you'd come back. Please tell me you have good news?"

"For the most part. Zeke, your request has been granted. If Quinn can get the hypnosis scripts to play for Gertie at night, you're allowed to jump into her experience. You're not allowed to talk, just to be present. Only to be seen if direly necessary, otherwise you are there for moral support. We agree that your energy and presence will help her. Also, you're allowed to be near her a few hours a day. Your cap is three hours throughout the day. Not all at once. Hopefully, this will help move the process on. She's more stubborn than *they* expected. Again, at no point can you talk, and you are to limit the visual connection. If *we* feel you're abusing this, *we* will take it away from you. Remember, *we*'re trying to help you and Gertie, not hurt you. *We* have our reasons of why this must be done certain ways."

Yes! I feel like a weight has been lifted from me. I can be around her again. Excitement flows through my body. "Not a problem, Gabe. I promise. I... well... I just need to be around her as much as she needs me."

Gabe smiles. "Yes, I know. You may go whenever you please. *We* have lifted the ban of her coming here also, but you can't bring her here. She has to come herself, and we feel she may with the scripts and experiences. This is her 'happy place', and that's usually where they go. Support her silently Zeke. You can do this. Help bring your girl peace."

Oh, I intend to.

A couple days later, I watch Quinn sneak into Gertie's room. She's been asleep for a while now, and I've been patiently, well not really, waiting for him. He changes the playlist to one he added earlier when she was in the shower. He stops, looks up, and sniffs. He then looks right over to the corner I'm in and smiles. He knows I'm here. My connection to Quinn has grown over the last few weeks. I really like the guy.

He waves to the room in general, I assume it's to me, and sneaks back out. The music transitions slowly and I hear Gertie's voice; she's speaking softly. It's something about relaxing your muscles and going down stairs while she counts backwards. I feel the shift in energy as she 'leaves' her body and goes into the trance state.

Showtime.

148

Chapter 23

Gertie

I'm floating. Staring out at a waterfall that looks familiar, I hear my own voice. Well, this is weird. I feel like I'm hypnotizing myself. How would I be doing that? You know what, I'm too tired to figure this out and this feels nice. You're a smart gal, shut your mind up, and listen. Yeah, that sounds good. I may have something smart to tell myself.

Looking down, I notice a fox and a raven at my feet. "Well, hello there. To what do I owe this pleasure?"

Smiling up at me, Fox says "Gertie it is time you allow us to help you. We have been your spirit animal guides all your life. We would help you from the sidelines, but now it is time we intervene. Yes, you can talk to animals, and they understand you. You have many special gifts in this life you haven't utilized. That is all about to change. Now come. Raven and I have some things to show you, and you have things to do."

Nodding, I follow. This seems crazy, yet interesting. I probably should be thinking this is a lot stranger than it is, but it feels right. Silently we move through a meadow full of lilies and wild daisies, all colors and sizes of my two favorite flowers. Raven flies beside us and circles us as we go. Reaching out, I touch the flowers as their scents linger in the air. Everything's so vivid and soft. It's colorful, yet without an edge.

Coming to the shore of a pond, I notice the lotus flowers and water lilies. I look to Fox, and he's looking out over the pond. I wait patiently for one of them to tell me what to do. Raven lands on my shoulder. I instinctively know that she's been there many times in my life. Her weight is familiar and comforting.

"Yes Gertie, I have been on your shoulder previously, and Fox has always been right by your side. You have often sensed us, but never acknowledged us.

We are guides meant to help you and protect you. Now is the time that you need both. It is time for you to shed your past. It is time for you to become vulnerable again. It is time for you to shed your protective walls. You have lived in a prison of your own making. One without love or happiness, and it has been carried with you through many lifetimes. This wall has been built up to proportions that cannot be knocked down alone. It must be deconstructed with help from our side of the realm."

I nod. "I think I understand. I've felt the walls. They are heavy and encompassing. I'm ready to let them go. The weight of carrying them has become too much for me. I have no clue how to do it. I don't know how to change. I don't know how to feel comfortable without their protection."

Fox nods. "Very good. I am glad that you are ready to change. This admission will help, as you will not fight to hold on to the walls. This process will not be an easy one, Gertie, but it is past time for it to be done. Are you ready, Gertie? Are you ready to allow happiness and love into your soul? Are you ready to shed your protective and dark walls?"

All I can think of in this moment is Zeke. I don't know how I could have love and happiness with him, but I need to focus on him if I want to accomplish this. He'll help me through this. I swear I feel him with us, also, but I can't see him.

Eagerly, I nod to Fox. "Yes. Please."

Raven points with her wing to the water's edge. "Gertie, do you notice the lotus flowers? Do you know that they, the beautiful lotus, rise from the mud and muck and are born new from what others consider to be ugliness and darkness? You, my child, are going to be the lotus. You live in ugliness. You live in self-inflected darkness, and it is time you are a Lotus once again."

Nodding, I quietly wait for more.

Raven continues. "You will go over to the waterfall and stand within the water. Do not be afraid, for it will not hurt you. The water will wash away the wall of protection you have built. In doing this, it will need to wash away all the ugliness you have experienced in your many lives. You built your walls out of your pain and grief, so each brick in the wall is an experience that needs to be washed away. You shall shut your eyes and let the water cleanse you. The hard part will be that you will, for just a moment, experience everything once again as it leaves. But do not try to hang on to it, do not let it break you from the water's spell. Stand and experience them. Release them to the water. Let them go. Can you do that, Gertie?"

"But that's the thing, I don't know how to let them go. What do I do?"

Fox turns to me. "You do not fight them. You need to experience them. You need to feel them, then you push through them to the other side of the experience. You are holding everything in. You do not deal with issues, you repress them. You must feel them, acknowledge them, and experience them to get rid of them. This is not easy to do and that is why most people repress them instead of experiencing them. They do not want to feel the raw emotions and pain. They prefer numbness, or the medicines that cut off the feelings, but this is wrong."

"To truly be able to move on, to release the negative, you must experience it. Gertie, you have many lifetimes to experience, thus why we are using the waterfall. This process will wash away a lot for you relatively quickly. Time is of the essence for you. You, yourself, chose this method for a client of yours while you were learning the craft of hypnotherapy. You know this works and how it works. Now, be open to this and let it work for you. Let it work for your love, who is waiting for you in the other realm."

Whipping my head around, my heart stops. "Zeke? Zeke is waiting for me? Why me?"

Fox nods. "Gertie. Zeke has been waiting for you because he loves you. You two are meant to spend eternity together. You have been searching for each other for many, many lifetimes. There is just this last block that needs released, and it is a large one. Let us now proceed. Go stand under the waterfall and remember to let everything go, no matter how painful the experiences may feel. Let yourself feel them, experience them, and then move to the next. You will be granted some messages at the end. That is your inner conscious, your intuitive side reminding your conscious brain of things you have known deep down all along, but have not remembered. Now, go. The time is now. We shall wait here."

Raven flies off my shoulder and sits on the ground next to Fox. Looking over to the waterfall, I start walking, slowly. I know this is what I need to do. It feels right. Hell, I've needed to do this for eons. I knew it when I got my hypnotherapy certificate. I did the program specifically to learn how to let things go since I knew I carried shit around too long. I was just too scared to do it. I didn't know how to live a different life. I never had a reason to force myself. If Fox is right, and Zeke's waiting for me to accomplish this, well then damnit, I'll do what I have to do to get to be with him again.

I walk to the water's edge, stop, and take a deep breath. I'm hesitant to go under, but know I will. For Zeke. Reaching my hand out into the water, an emotional zap runs through my body that brings me to my knees. I look over toward Raven and Fox for guidance, or maybe support. They nod. I stand up and step forward.

My body fills with sensations. Tingling. Buzzing. Pain. Agony. Sadness. Cold. Warmth. Electricity. Vibrations. Frustration. Anger. Shutting my eyes, I let my head fall back slightly, the water hits my forehead, and hairline, and continues down over me. Repeating to myself, "I can do this. I can do this." I picture Zeke and gain the strength to endure the flashes of memories, the sensations, the emotions, and the pain flowing through my body. It's like a movie through centuries of life time's running through my head. Seeing nothing for longer than what feels like a nanosecond, it moves so fast, like I'm in the eye of a tornado. Emotions are changing quicker and quicker; I try not to focus on one particular thing. Letting the memories fill me with emotions that feel foreign to me, I don't fight it as I picture Zeke.

Eventually, the memories start to slow, the emotions stay a little longer for each, and my pain is raw and intense, my body exhausted, yet my soul feeling lighter than ever before. My body is no longer numb. I feel tingles and vibrations through my arms and legs; a new liveliness has awakened inside me. I can feel my blood pumping through my body. I actually *feel* something.

The last memory plays in slow motion. There's a man, in a loin cloth, being dragged by two other men. All of them dirty and dark skinned from being in the sun too long. Their hair is scraggly and down their backs with beards about the same length. They're carrying him with his arms over their shoulders; he appears to be unconscious. Blood is running down his body. A woman is screaming in the mouth of a cave while holding a little baby. She is crying and crying. I feel the sharp stab of pain in my heart and immediately feel nauseous. The pain is so intense I feel like I can't breathe. She is desperate; she is scared. Instantly, I start crying. I know this pain. I know this family. That was my pain.

That is me, holding our baby, my heart being ripped from my body as those men leave with the love of my life. The man is Zeke. We were a family.

Sensing arms wrapping around me, I continue to shudder and sob. I can't stop crying. This was the moment my soul broke, never to be healed. This is why Zeke filled the emptiness in my soul. He is my missing piece. The puzzle piece missing for centuries is now filled. No one else even came close.

There was never anything wrong with me. It was never that I was unlovable, like I believed, it was that I was never letting another close again. I was too afraid of losing someone else. Zeke was right, I was the one doing this to myself. I can be loved. He did love me back then, which means he can still love me now, right?

Finally, the crying stops. Calming down, I notice I'm sitting behind the waterfall. Fox is by my side and Raven is on my shoulder. I still feel arms around me even though I'm now sitting on the ground. I feel encompassed in the warmth.

Fox looks me directly in the eye. "You did wonderfully, Gertie. Perfect. We are so proud of you. Did you get any clarity during the cleansing?"

"I'm not sure I got a lot of clarity, Fox, but I got a very important revelation. I feel so much lighter. I feel… well I don't know how to explain it, but freer, more open, lighter. I don't feel as heavy, or dark, or weighted down as I did before."

Raven nods. "That is good, my child. How does your heart feel?"

"My heart feels lighter, also. It feels hopeful. I want to say it's open, but it's already full of Zeke, so there is no more room for anyone. But it's open to him. If that makes any kind of sense."

"It does my child. For your soul, it makes complete sense. The time for you to return has come. This has been an intense and powerful experience. We are so very proud of you. Please remember, over the next couple days, you may be overly emotional as memories continue to release and be remembered. You may have flashes of these memories that induce changes in your emotions. Let them play out. Remember, you must experience them to release them. Do you understand?"

"Yes, Raven, I understand. Will you both still be with me?"

"Yes. We are always with you, my child. Talk to us whenever you need. You do not have to voice anything aloud, think it and we will hear. We will answer you in whatever way is best at that time. Now, you must go back."

Walking away, I take a nice deep breath and smile. Coffee and mocha. Zeke is here. My heart is now content.

I awake the next morning to a silent room. Why isn't my white noise playing? Looking over at my phone, I see a blank screen. I look around the room. Something's different. Everything looks the same, but it feels...different. I feel different. Stretching and rubbing my eyes I notice a lighter feeling throughout my body. Where's Freddie? What the hell is going on?

Stumbling out of bed, flashes of a dream come back to me. It wasn't of Zeke, but...animals? A waterfall? And why the hell do I remember a lotus flower? What did I eat before bed last night? I'm all out of whack and almost, content?

I really need some coffee. Rubbing my eyes, I grab my phone and head toward the door of my room. Checking my phone to see how late I slept, I notice the white noise app I go to sleep to is closed. Looking at a hypnosis track on the screen, my head's all foggy and confused. Why is that up? Wait, is this the waterfall releasing script I wrote?

Vivid memories now flood back to me. Am I remembering a fox and a black bird, a raven maybe? They're talking to me. And a waterfall. Washing down over me. Falling backwards on the beanbag as flashes of the dream run through my mind, I'm there again. Standing under the waterfall, feeling the pain and emotions pulse through my body. Sitting perfectly still, I stare at the floor. I remember everything. Zeke. A baby. A family. Love. Desperation. Sadness. Relief.

A sob breaks free from my chest. It's been ages since I've cried like this, but I remember Raven telling me to let it go. Lying back into the beanbag, I curl up into a fetal position to hold myself while the tears stream down my face. This is the first time I have cried alone, without Freddie, in a decade. It's strange, but I know not to fight it. I sense arms and warmth around me, same as in my dream last night, and even though I'm crying, I smile. It's soothing. Zeke. He's here, and he's supporting me.

As the tears dry up, I can speak again. "I love you, Zeke. I promise to do anything I need to do so we can be together again someday. Please, please, wait for me."

An hour later I pull myself out of my beanbag and shower. Standing there letting the water wash over me as it did in my dream last night, it feels so good. Refreshing and cleansing. I take time to notice the feel of the water on my skin, the smell of the soap, and the smooth, soft feel of the soap on my skin. Things I've never taken time before to enjoy. If someone asked me before what my soap smelled like, I wouldn't have been able to answer them.

Everything is more alive to me. I'm noticing more color, more detail in the bathroom, and the weird pattern on the shower curtain. I couldn't have told you if we had a shower curtain before, let alone what was on it.

Heading to the kitchen for much needed coffee, I notice it's already noon. Picking up a note from Quinn, I see he won't be back until supper time. He also took Freddie out this morning since I was 'dead to the world'. Looking around the room, I spot Freddie curled up sleeping with Petunia on their bed, in the living room. He usually wakes up immediately when I come out in the mornings and runs over for pets and love.

Sitting down next to him, I pet his soft fur. It feels like silk. He curls closer to me but doesn't open his eyes. He sighs and snuggles. Well, okay then. I guess my stress energy's real low. That's the only time he isn't right by my side. This poor dog's been through the ringer with me all these years. My stress and anxiety couldn't have been good for him. I'm so lucky to have this little bugger.

Knowing I should let him sleep, I pick him up and cuddle him to my chest, anyway. Rubbing my nose and cheek on the top of his head, I feel peaceful.

"Oh, Freddie boy. I love you so much. I hope you know that. You've been my rock the whole time you've been with me. I hope you know how much I appreciate you. You're my little Lovebug!" I whisper into his ears. Opening his eyes, he licks my nose and snuggles his head up under my chin. There's nothing better in the world than a dog's unconditional love.

My heart swells with love and warmth, both foreign to me, but not unwanted now. I'm so happy to have cuddle time with Freddie. Sitting on the floor for a half an hour, Freddie and I snuggle together. It's like he senses the change in me, too. He seems happier and lighter. I hope I wasn't bringing him down. Putting him down next to Petunia, he curls back in with her as I walk to the couch and pick up my laptop. In the shower, I had a perfect idea for another book.

Opening my laptop, I scan through my email. Nothing out of the ordinary today, thankfully. Bob emailed the sales reports from last month, and that the company wants me to do a book signing. Huh. Maybe I'll say, yes, finally. I'm feeling so much better that it might not be a bad thing.

Starting a new word document, I type out my ideas for Quinn and Roman's book. I'll have to think of new names for the characters, but I'm determined to give those boys a happy ending. They'd be perfect together if Quinn could get his shit together, and if Roman would get over his guilt.

Three hours later, I stop taking notes and make supper. Pulling a frozen lasagna out of the freezer, I preheat the oven and set the table before popping it in the oven. Salad? Sure, why not.

By the time it's all ready to put on the table, Quinn walks in the door. "Well, what do we have here? Susie Housemaker's being domestic?"

Chuckling, my smile reaches my eyes for once. "Yes. I'm hungry and felt like being nice. Come my lovely, sit and I shall feed you."

My lord. Have I always been this cheesy? Yes, Yes, I do believe I have. I'm completely okay with this revelation.

Looking at me quizzically, he tilts his head, "What's going on here? What's changed?"

He waves his hand all over and around my area, dramatically. It provokes a full-on belly laugh. I don't think I've ever done that before so I'm not really sure. Now Quinn's eyes are large and bugging out of his head. "Ok, now you're just freaking me the hell out. Seriously, are you ok?"

Once I get my giggling under control, which takes another minute or more, I nod my head. "I'm good Quinn, better than good. I don't know how it happened, but sometime in my sleep last night, one of my hypnotherapy scripts started playing on my phone, and I had an amazing experience with it. It changed something in me. I feel lighter and...well, happy. You wouldn't know anything about that, would you? I mean, I can't believe that this script would just start playing out of nowhere without help."

Giving him a stern look and trying not to laugh, I know he did it. He's been hounding me for weeks to try to change, to open up, and talk to him. He even suggested a journal because he was worried about me. That one freaked me out! That's so not Quinn.

"Nope. Have no clue." Quinn tries desperately to keep a straight face, but his left eye ticks as he speaks. That's his tell. He's lying.

"Liar."

"I love you too much to lie to you, Gertie, don't you know that by now?"

"I love you too, Quinn. Enough to let it slide this time, because I feel great. But remember, revenge, even good revenge, can be a bitch, my love."

He smirks, clearly not worried by my threat. "What's for supper, chickie?"

Dishing out the food, he tells me about his day. I'll let him get away with the topic change for now, knowing he did it for my own good, but his day will come. I'm glad he did it, but I'll never tell him. I'm going to make him sweat waiting for revenge. I have more than enough ways to play dirty, too.

After supper, finishing the dishes, Quinn goes for a shower. Not feeling like TV, I decide to listen to an audio book in my room. Pulling my earphones out of the drawer next to my bed, I prop myself up on a pillow. I've had headache on and off all day. Popping another pain reliever, I settle in and get comfortable. Scrolling through my favorites, I pick one of my favorite books. It was just released on audio last week, so I'm anxious to listen to it. I've read it many times, but I really like the narrator's voice; it's deep and soothing. Settling in with Freddie on my lap, I shut my eyes. Today's been the best day I can remember.

No better way to end the day than a good book, and the love and warmth of my beloved best fur friend. My heart is full, content, and complete for the first time ever.

Epilogue

Gertie

Waking up, everything's bright and colorful. Something smells like chocolate coffee. I love that smell. Coffee and mocha. Zeke. Looking around as I'm lying in grass by a waterfall, I recognize it immediately. I've been here before. Often actually, just not recently. My heart speeds up, and I feel like I am vibrating with excitement.

Then I see him. Zeke's on the bench, in our spot, a couple feet away, staring out past the field of wildflowers watching the waterfall. His hands are behind his head, and his legs are stretched out in front of him, crossed at the ankles. He's relaxed and looks like he's patiently waiting for something. He looks solid, real, not transparent and luminescent as he had been. I look down and see that I'm also solid. I pinch myself. It doesn't hurt, but does leave a mark on my skin. That means only one thing, I'm dead.

Walking over to the bench, I sit beside him. He smiles, but his gaze is still aimed at the water. I touch Zeke's arm and feel his skin. Our first touch. Feeling a zap of energy go through me, warmth, and relaxation flows through my body.

Is it possible? Can I hope to stay here with him and be happy forever, finally?

"What happened this time? Why am I here? Can I be excited to stay? Please, Zeke?"

Zeke turns towards me as his smile widens. It's slightly sad, yet has a hint of hopefulness, also. His eyes shine bright green like I've never seen before. The dimple appears, and my chest pings with electricity.

"You died in your sleep, Gertie. It was an aneurysm in your brain. It ruptured while you slept, and you transitioned quietly. You felt nothing? You haven't had any symptoms?"

"No, I didn't feel anything, but I'd been having headaches. I remember listening to an audio book and fell asleep. Then woke up here, smelling you."

Looking around again, hope is blooming in my chest. "So, this time, I don't go back? I can stay here, and be happy with you?" I ask eagerly, needing him to confirm. I need to hear the words.

"No, Gertie, you don't go back. Your time has come. Are you ok with that? Wait, my smell? You still smell it up here?"

Thinking for a minute, I ask myself; am I ok staying here with Zeke? Heck yeah. This isn't even a question I have to think about. The only people that will miss me are Quinn, and my parents, maybe Shelly too. The thought of Quinn sends a scare through me.

"You smell like coffee and mocha. I thought I told you that before. Yes, I smelled it as soon as I opened my eyes. Ironically, my two favorite things. And yes, I'm ok with it, more than ok, actually. I'm excited to be here with you. This is where I'm meant to be. What will happen to Quinn? He has no one now. Will he be ok? Will he take care of Freddie for me?"

Zeke looks at me blankly, then laughs. "I knew I should've made a bet with Gabe about Quinn and Freddie." Shaking his head, he looks back at me. "Yes, Quinn will take care of Freddie. And I love that I smell like your two favorite things. I like to hear you say it, because it kind of makes me way too happy. I've missed you so much. Gertie, it's killed me not to be able to connect with you, you know that, right?"

Looking out over the water, I think about that question. "Zeke, for the first couple months, you were the only thing that made me happy. You felt like my missing piece. You filled the empty space inside me, the loneliness. Then, you were gone, and I hated it. I felt incomplete again, and wasn't sure how to adapt. I was frustrated and depressed. I had no idea how to get you back into my life. I am, finally, here with you and have the chance to stay forever by your side, the way we were supposed to be from the very beginning, since that lifetime when you were taken from me. I've been searching for you for centuries. I realize all of this now. But no, before my dream last night, I had no clue how you felt. I was never good at picking those types of things up because of all the walls I had surrounding me. I could see it between others, but not for me. I missed you, too, Zeke. Way too much."

Smiling, he nods. "I've been communicating with Quinn for the last couple weeks. He decided to try the hypnosis. Gabe told me before you got here *they*, again, whoever *they* are, decided you'd have that dream with or without the hypnosis. *They* knew that today was your last day. *They*'d set everything in motion with your accident, but *they* didn't think you'd fight so much. So, *they* planned for you to have the experience with your guides. Gabe got me permission to be there with you. We thought it would help you finally let go. I hope it did. It meant a lot to me to be there with you, Gertie. We are one. You make me whole. I don't ever want to go back to just being a lost half."

Smiling at him, I vibrate with excitement. "Me either, Zeke. Once they told me you were waiting for me, nothing could have stopped me. It all made sense once I saw where we started. I knew that was you and me. On one hand it broke me, again, to know what happened, yet at the same time it put me back together. The knowledge filled all the cracks in my heart. I knew we were meant to find each other again, that we were each other's missing piece. I promise you, Zeke, we'll never go back to being a half. We're a full whole now, and that will never change."

Putting his arm around my shoulders, he pulls me tight against him. Sighing, I melt into him. I can feel his breath on the top of my head, his side pressing up against mine, his leg touching mine, and the soul is once again sealed. We'd never be apart.

"Now, you didn't answer my question. I need to know about Quinn. I know he'll take care of Freddie. My parents and sister will take care of each other. Who will take care of Quinn? He's been my lifeline, and I've been his all our life. I can't leave him hanging. He's a strong person, but he needs a support system. He has no one, Zeke."

"Ok, formal stuff first. You do have a choice. You get to decide what you want to do next. You can either go back to human form as a baby, you can become a 'helper' to someone in need to help them find their way in life, kind of like I did with you, although, I didn't have a choice, or you can move on to the next realm, which you've proven is where you ultimately belong. Choice is up to you."

Thinking over the choices, I stare out at the waterfall. Listening to the water helps me think and process it all.

"So, I hear the choices, and trust me, there will be NO returning to the earthly realm. Nope. Nada. Ain't going to do it ever again, if possible. Moving on to the next realm sounds awesome, but that still doesn't answer my question about Quinn."

Zeke looks sad for a second before responding, "You can choose who you want to help if you become a helper. Humans like to think of them as angels, as you did with me. You can stay and help Quinn before moving on."

This sends a thrill of anticipation through me. Images of all the possibilities of how I can help Quinn roll through my mind. Looking at Zeke, I realize I've been in love with this soul since our soul's inception. It's been centuries of searching for each other again, I'm doing nothing without him.

He's who and what I've been searching for over spans of time. Now that I can finally be with him, touch him, how could I be without him? I can't. There's no question about it, but I can't leave Quinn without knowing that he's going to be ok. I can't have him end up the lost soul Zeke was if I can stay and help. My heart hurts; it's breaking all over again. I love them both in such different ways. I don't think I can chose.

"Zeke, what'll happen to you if I stay and help Quinn? Will we be separated? I can't do that. I just found you; I will not survive looking for you for centuries, again. I love you, and I love Quinn. I don't want to leave Quinn helpless, but I can't lose you either. Is there any way we can help him together?"

He blows out a breath and smiles. I feel his body relaxing against mine. "I was so scared you wouldn't think about adding me in your decision." Turning to me, he grabs my hands.

"I'm allowed to stay with you and help, also, if you chose. I'm stalled in my soul's evolution, by my own choice. I don't want to be without you, either. I know I couldn't handle it. Look what I did in this last life. It took us forever to find each other, and that was with help. I won't go through that again. My future belongs to you. I give my soul, my future, and my heart to you completely. I'm letting you make the decision of what WE do. If you choose to include me, then I want to be the other part of your soul forever. I'm willing to do whatever you want, as long as we can be together, Gertie. Is that what you want?"

Tears are streaming down my face. I feel true happiness. I truly feel loved. Someone wants to be with me. They'll do anything to be by my side. I don't even have to think about my answer.

"Of course! There's no doubt in my mind, or my heart. You're it. You're my other half. You're my future. I've said it multiple times, and I'll keep saying it; I've never felt complete till you barged into my coma and became a part of my life. Can we please stay and help Quinn? You don't mind helping him? He needs peace, Zeke. He deserves to find peace. He needs to find his love and finally get some happiness in his life, too. I don't think I could rest in the next realm without helping him."

Zeke pulls me into his arms, and then up onto his lap for a huge full body hug. It's all I've been dreaming about it. His touch finally brings me peace, a calm I've never felt except with him. I finally feel complete. I'm home. Our energy blends and melds together; we're one again.

Snuggling into my neck, Zeke whispers to me, "Yes. We can do that, my love. Uh, I know I mentioned this before, but is it wrong that I'm completely happy that you associate your two favorite smells with me? This really makes me, well, kind of speechless, actually."

Giggling, I wiggle as his breath tickles my neck. "It isn't wrong at all. I think it's quite appropriate. All three things make me happy: coffee, mocha, and you. Everything I ever needed is in you."

We sit in silent contentment holding each other and reconnecting our energies. His hands stroke up and down on my back in a soothing motion. A light breeze is blowing around us bringing the smell of the flowers. We listen to the waterfall and just be.

"Hey, wait. You mentioned someone named Gabe. Who's that?"

"Actually, I have no clue what he's considered. He's like me, only he helps lost souls on this side. I don't know if he helps humans or just souls. He came to me while I was struggling. *They* wouldn't let me see you, and I wasn't dealing well. He explained everything to me that you saw in your dream. He got me permission to communicate with Quinn, and he is who's been keeping me updated on you since *they* wouldn't let me visit you. Basically, he kept me sane and helped me evolve at the same time."

"That makes sense. I see how a lost soul would need someone in this realm to help him. I think I like him, already, considering he helped you."

We're both quiet as I think about my dream and everything I learned. I try to internalize as much as possible, as a thought hits me.

"Hey, whose soul was our baby in that lifetime so long ago? I was holding a baby in that memory."

Smiling even larger, he laughs. "You didn't figure that one out? I'm surprised. You're usually really good at picking up energies, and you didn't notice?"

"Nope, I was too locked on you. I didn't pay attention to anything else. I didn't realize there was a baby till now, really. Who was it? Apparently, someone I know if you're acting this way!"

Chuckling, he bops me on the nose. "That soul's been with you in every life you've lived, in some form or another. Once he passes from this life he's currently living, he'll join us. Think about it for a minute, and see if you can pick it out. Who's the other you asked about earlier?"

I know it isn't Quinn. He would've been obvious to me. Who did I mention earlier?

"Oh, holy crap! It's Freddie? Really?"

Zeke nods his head. "He's been everything from a pet, to a sibling, to a parent to you over the centuries. *They* always send him to protect you. That's why he was a baby in that lifetime, *they* knew those men wouldn't kill, or take you from a child. Freddie's always been your protector. Once he transitions from this life, he'll join us. He's your guardian angel."

I should've known that. Freddie's been a soul mate through this life. I can't wait to see him again and for him to join us. I wonder what form he will take over here?

After a while longer of cuddling and relaxing, I hear the light sound of a bell. Zeke sighs. "It's time my love. Your transition and coping period are complete. Stand up, sweetie."

Scooching off his lap and standing, I hold out my hand to help him up. Standing, he wraps me in his arms and gives me the kiss we've been waiting on for centuries. It's perfection. The feelings of being whole with this soul again, is beyond reality. It is everything.

"Time for what Zeke? What happens now?"

"It's time for us to experience the happiness we deserve, and to help others find theirs. Finally, Gertie, finally, we get to be together forever."

The End

About the Author

Who am I? Good question. I'm a middle-aged girl who has always wanted to bring the stories that float around in my head to life. I love to people watch and tend to come up with a story for every person I see. I'm married and love to drive my husband crazy by singing loudly, and badly, at the top of my lungs in the car. I love animals, especially my two fur-kids, Ginger Lou and Charlie. I have multiple college degrees that I don't use while I design playgrounds full-time instead. My desire is to make people laugh daily and to help others in any way I can. I openly admit to having a strange sense of humor and hope that others enjoy it. I love telling stories full of humor and happy endings. I'm a firm believer in three mottos: Be the change you want to see in the world, be careful what you wish for as the Universe will provide it, and Love is Love. I love coffee more than life, with chocolate coming in a close second. Oh, but I do love my husband and family, too. When I'm not working, reading, or writing, I'm probably dressed in my comfy tie-dye t-shirt playing epic games of fetch with Charlie from my oversized beanbag.

Acknowledgements

Gertie was a labor of love for me, as well as a dream come true. She has been renting space in my head for at least a decade. It was way past time to get her out of my head and into the pages of this book.

I've wanted to write a novel since I was in high school. I never allowed myself time to sit down and do it until October 2017 when I joined NaNo, thanks to Michael. Kyleen added me to a Facebook NaNo group of wonderful people who all supported and encouraged each other. My Wonder Writers have been such an inspiration. We have learned so much from each other, and I have gained a lot of new friends.

Ashe, Stephanie, Abigail, Jacki, Jill, Nora and Michele, you gals especially have been there for me almost every step of the way and answered enough annoying questions to get a huge THANK YOU from me. You all have been my rocks and my cheerleaders through this time. I appreciate it more than you know.

My poor husband and dogs have had to put up with me through these months of self-doubt, my muttering to myself as I wrote or edited, and some nights where I totally ignored them. I have many games of fetch to catch up on with Charlie. And Hubs, you have been more than supportive; I love you for putting up with me and encouraging me in this wild dream.

Lastly, to my beloved Petey, who we lost last year- I based Freddie off you buddy. You were a soul-mate of mine and we had an unusual connection. You always were my unofficial therapy dog, and I will love you forever for that little buddy.

Find me on Facebook:
https://www.facebook.com/lacieminier

My website: lacieminier.com

Made in the USA
Middletown, DE
06 February 2023

23340264R00102